THE SECRET WARNING

STRANGE events involve Frank and Joe Hardy in a mystery which shrouds an ancient treasure—the golden head of the Pharaoh Rhamaton IV. First, a cryptic unsigned warning from Egypt; second, the ghost of a bloodthirsty pirate of the eighteenth century, who, according to legend, haunted nearby Whalebone Island years ago and recently has reappeared.

The owner of the million-dollar golden Pharaoh's head claims it was aboard the freighter *Katawa,* which sank not far from Whalebone Island. But suspicious developments indicate that Mehmet Zufar may be trying to defraud the shipping line's insurance company. Frank and Joe enthusiastically accept the challenge of their famous detective father to assist him in investigating the complex case for Transmarine Underwriters.

A puzzling clue leads the Hardys to Whalebone Island, where they almost lose their lives in a violent explosion. Someone desperately wants to get rid of them. But who? Is it the ghostly pirate?

Frank and Joe's perilous scuba-diving search in the ocean depths off the island yields electrifying discoveries that cap the climax of this exciting mystery.

A chill of fear struck the Hardys as they approached the trapped diver

Hardy Boys Mystery Stories

THE SECRET
WARNING

BY

FRANKLIN W. DIXON

NEW YORK
GROSSET & DUNLAP
Publishers

LIBRARY OF CONGRESS CATALOG CARD NUMBER: 66-12695

ISBN: 0-448-08917-3 (TRADE EDITION)

ISBN: 0-448-18917-8 (LIBRARY EDITION)

PRINTED IN THE UNITED STATES OF AMERICA

CONTENTS

CHAPTER I

A Ghost Walks

A LOUD ring of the doorbell startled the Hardy boys as they sat watching a TV mystery. Joe tuned down the volume. "Who could that be at this time of night?" the blond, seventeen-year-old youth wondered aloud.

"Maybe a client of Dad's. It can't be Mom and Aunt Gertrude—they have a key." Frank, dark-haired and a year older than his brother, got up and strode to the door.

A telegraph messenger was standing on the front porch. "Cablegram for Fenton Hardy."

Frank signed for the message and took it back to the living room. "For Dad," he reported. "Coming from overseas, this may be urgent."

"We'd better open it," Joe suggested.

Frank slit the yellow envelope and read the contents. "Good grief!" he exclaimed. " *'Beware the Pharaoh's head. Doom to all who seek it!'* "

"The Pharaoh's head? What does that mean?"

Frank shrugged. "Search me."

"Well, who sent it?"

"I don't know that, either," Frank said, perplexed. "There's no name on the message, but it came from Cairo, Egypt."

Joe took the cablegram, studied it intently, then hurried out to the hallway telephone and called the local telegraph office. When he hung up, he frowned in puzzlement.

Frank, coming into the hall, queried, "What did they say?"

"The message was received just that way—unsigned. Apparently there's no rule requiring a sender to include his name."

"I think we'd better contact Dad right away," Frank decided.

Fenton Hardy, formerly a detective in the New York City Police Department, had retired to the seaside town of Bayport and soon had become nationally known as a crack private investigator. His two sons, Frank and Joe, who had inherited their father's sleuthing talents, often helped out on his cases.

The boys hurried upstairs to switch on the powerful short-wave radio in the detective's study. Mr. Hardy always carried a compact transceiver in order to be able to communicate with his home in cases of emergency.

Frank beamed out the usual code call repeatedly. But the only response was a jumble of static.

"He must be away from his hotel, or wherever he's staying," Joe said.

"Could be." Frank glanced at the window as a flash of lightning brought an extra loud crackle from the speaker. "Or maybe we're not getting through. That storm brewing out there may be interfering with our transmission."

After a few more minutes, the boys gave up for the time being and went back downstairs. A loud clap of thunder sounded as they reached the living room.

"Boy, looks as if we're in for a real cloudburst," Frank remarked anxiously. "I sure hope Mom and Aunt Gertrude don't get caught in it."

He was about to resume his seat in front of the television when he heard Joe gasp.

"Thought I saw something at the window."

Frank stared quizzically at his brother. "You mean a person—or what?"

"I don't know," Joe said. "It was just a fleeting impression. May have been my imagination. Is the prowler alarm on?"

"Not yet. Mom said to leave it off till they got home." Frank added with a grin, "You know Aunt Gertrude—she'd really pin our ears back if the alarm system went off just as they were coming up to the house."

Joe chuckled as he imagined his tall, peppery aunt's reaction to being caught in a blaze of floodlights, accompanied by a shattering alarm signal. "Think I'll take a look outside, anyhow," he told Frank. "It won't hurt to make sure."

Joe was just starting into the hallway when the doorbell rang. "Now what?" he muttered as he switched on the porch light. He yanked open the front door. A man stood clutching a cane. He wore a felt hat and Navy officer's raincoat.

"Captain Early! Welcome aboard, sir!"

The man's ruddy, weather-beaten face broke into a wide grin. "Howdy, Joe!" He saluted and gave the boy's hand a brisk squeeze as he limped inside.

Hearing their voices, Frank hurried to greet the visitor. "Dad will be sorry he missed you," he said as they shook hands.

Captain Phil "Pearly" Early was an old friend of the Hardys. Now retired, he lived alone in a house on the coast, north of Barmet Bay, and devoted his time to writing books on sea lore.

"I probably should have phoned," the captain apologized, "but I had to come to Bayport on an errand, anyhow, so I took a chance." He doffed his hat and coat, revealing a crisp gray crew cut and a slight but wiry build.

As Joe took his things, there came the sudden sound of a drenching downpour. Rain pelted the roof and splattered against the windows.

"You got here just in time," Frank said.

Captain Early nodded and tapped his thigh. "Hurricane weather. My game leg always tells me when we're in for a blow." His ruddy face turned serious. "By the way, did you boys just have a visitor?"

Frank shook his head. "No, sir. Why?"

"When my taxi drew up here, I saw a man standing just outside the hedge around your grounds. He darted off as the headlights beamed on him."

Joe exchanged a quick, startled glance with his brother. "What did he look like?"

"Rather odd," said Captain Early. "I suppose that's really why I mentioned him. He had a black cloak or coat, a bushy red beard, and—well, something strange about the eyes."

The boys escorted their visitor into the living room. As Frank turned off the TV, Captain Early asked, "You fellows home alone?"

"We are just now," Joe replied. "Mom and Aunt Gertrude have gone to a concert." Seeing the captain's thoughtful frown, he added, "Did you want to see Dad, sir?"

"As a matter of fact, I did. But I might as well put the case in your hands."

Frank settled eagerly into a chair. "You have a mystery you want investigated?"

The captain nodded as he filled his pipe. "Doesn't amount to much, probably, but all the same I'd like to know what's behind it. Twice recently, my house has been broken into at night."

"Was anything stolen?" Joe inquired.

"No, because both times I woke up and scared the intruder off." The first time, Captain Early related, his study had been ransacked. On the second occasion, the burglar had come into his bedroom.

"Did you see him well enough to give us a description?" put in Frank.

"No, I hardly saw him at all. By the time I switched on the light, he was out the window and away over the back porch roof."

"When did this happen?" Joe asked.

"The first time was on Friday, and the second attempt was just last night—Sunday."

Frank said, "Any idea what the thief was after?"

"None at all. I never keep any large amount of money in the house." Captain Early puffed on his pipe for a moment. "Incidentally, I've had a strange feeling of being followed several times lately—including tonight on my way to Bayport. But that may be pure bosh."

Again the boys exchanged glances. Captain Early, with his brilliant war record, was certainly not a man given to fearful flights of imagination.

"Jumpin' Jupiter, you really *have* given us a

mystery to work on," said Joe. "Have you told the police about the break-ins?"

"Yes, but naturally there wasn't much they could do, except check for fingerprints—and there weren't any."

"Look," Frank said. "We were trying to contact Dad earlier on another matter. Suppose I try again."

Leaving Joe to entertain their guest, Frank hurried to the short-wave set in their father's study. This time, his code call brought an immediate response. Mr. Hardy, speaking from Philadelphia, explained that he and his operative, Sam Radley, had just returned to their hotel.

When Frank mentioned the mysterious cablegram, the sleuth reacted with keen interest. "That message relates to the case we're working on, son, and it could provide an important lead. I'll fill you and Joe in on all the details as soon as I return."

Next, Frank told about Captain Early's visit.

"Hmm. Certainly sounds as if something more is involved than an ordinary case of breaking and entering," Mr. Hardy said. "But there's not much I can do from here. You and Joe will have to handle it for the time being. Say, there is *one* thing you can do for me."

"Yes, Dad?"

"Ask Captain Early what he knows about the legend of Whalebone Island."

Mystified, Frank signed off and returned to the

living room. At the mention of Whalebone Island, Captain Early's ruddy face paled.

"Great Scott!" he exclaimed. *"It can't be!"*

"What's wrong, sir?" Frank asked.

The Navy man hesitated before replying. "Whalebone Island, as you probably know, lies off the coast, south of here. In colonial days it was the hideout of a ruthless pirate named Red Rogers. Of course you've heard the term 'Jolly Roger'?"

Frank said, "The skull and crossbones?"

"Right. And the same name was sometimes given to Red Rogers because of his bloodthirsty sense of humor."

Captain Early went on slowly, "Red Rogers always wore a black cloak and had a bushy red beard and a scar which pulled down the corner of one eye."

"Wow!" Joe gasped. "Just like that fellow you saw outside tonight!"

Captain Early nodded. "Exactly. After Rogers was killed in a sea fight, the island was pretty much avoided. In fact, it was said to be haunted."

At that moment the captain's story was interrupted by a flash of lightning, followed by a deafening clap of thunder which seemed to shake the whole house. A second later the darkness outside was lit up by a blinding flash of lightning.

"Look!" Joe yelled and pointed.

A red-bearded figure in a black cloak was peering through the window!

A ghostly figure was peering through the window!

CHAPTER II

Close Combat

THE lightning flickered out, and the ghostly figure was gone almost instantly. Frank and Joe leaped to their feet and rushed to the front door, followed by Captain Early hobbling on his cane.

Ignoring the gusty torrents of rain, the boys dashed out into the stormy darkness and around the corner of the house. Not a soul was in sight. The Hardys separated to search the whole yard, but even when another jagged flash of lightning lit up the night with daylike brilliance they could see no sign of the figure which had appeared at the window.

"It's hopeless!" Frank groaned. "Let's get back inside before we drown!"

Drenched to the skin, the brothers changed into dry clothes before resuming their conversation with Captain Early.

"Did anyone live on Whalebone Island in those

old days that you were telling us about?" Frank asked.

"No, except for fishermen who camped there overnight or put up temporary huts from time to time. I suppose the stories of ghosts on the island may have arisen because members of Red Rogers' crew were said to be returning there secretly."

"Maybe to dig up buried treasure!" put in Joe.

"Possibly," the Navy man agreed with a smile. "Or fugitives from the law may have hidden there occasionally. At any rate, the spooky legends of Jolly Roger and his cutthroats finally died out, and sometime in the eighteen-hundreds a lighthouse was erected on Whalebone Island. Then, in the closing days of World War II, a lighthouse keeper there named Tang went out of his mind."

"How come?" Frank asked.

Captain Early gave a shrug. "He claimed the island was being haunted again by Red Rogers' ghost. More likely, he'd just cracked up under the loneliness and isolation, I suppose. Anyhow, soon after that the lighthouse was closed down."

"Because of what happened to Tang?" Joe asked.

"No, no. The equipment was outdated and a new light, much more powerful, had been built on Dory Point to serve that same general coastal area."

"What's on the island now?" Frank inquired.

"Nothing. It's abandoned as far as I know."

The brothers were greatly intrigued. Any hint of mystery attracted them, and many times had plunged them into exciting sleuthing adventures. One of their first had been locating *The Tower Treasure*. Recently, they had successfully uncovered the secret of *A Figure in Hiding*.

Captain Early tucked his pipe into his pocket. "Well, boys, it's been a pleasant visit, but I'd better be starting back. As a matter of fact, this is far later than I intended to linger in town."

The navy officer explained that he had had motor trouble while driving to Bayport. "I had to call for a tow car from a garage. That's why I arrived here by taxi. By the way, may I use your phone?"

"Of course. Help yourself," Frank replied.

The captain checked with the garage and hung up, frowning. "Drat the luck, my car needs a new distributor, and they can't get one till morning."

Frank and Joe immediately urged Captain Early to stay overnight. Grateful but embarrassed, he accepted. Frank showed the captain to the first-floor guest room and laid out pajamas and bathrobe, while Joe wrote a note to his mother and aunt telling them about the unexpected overnight guest. He stuck it on the hall mirror.

Then the boys went upstairs to bed, leaving only a hallway light burning for their mother and Aunt Gertrude. Soon the household was dark and silent, except for the steady patter of the rain.

Some time later Frank awoke with a start. From below came confused sounds, topped by a shrill angry voice and punctuated by the sudden clash of china being broken. The latter noise roused Joe.

"Good night!" he muttered. "What's going on?"

"That's Aunt Gertrude's voice!" Frank exclaimed. "Come on! We'd better get down there!"

The boys dashed downstairs, almost colliding with their slim, attractive mother, who was on her way up.

"What's wrong, Mom?" Joe cried out.

"G-g-goodness, I hardly know!" Mrs. Hardy stammered. "Somebody peeked out of our guest room as we entered the house, and Aunt Gertrude went after him."

Gulping with dismay, Frank and Joe ran to the scene of combat.

"Take that, you scoundrel!" they heard Aunt Gertrude shriek. "I'll teach you to break into houses."

Frank groped for the wall switch and instantly the guest room was ablaze with light. Captain

Early was backing toward a closet, striving to protect himself, while the boys' tall, angular maiden aunt poked at him with her wet umbrella.

"Aunt Gertrude! Please!" Frank exclaimed. "This is Captain Early—our guest!"

"Oh, my goodness, it *is!*" said Aunt Gertrude, adjusting her spectacles. "Why on earth didn't you say so?"

"Madam, I've been trying to," the captain replied, slipping into his bathrobe.

He explained that when he had heard footsteps in the hall, he thought it might have been the intruder they had seen at the window.

"So I peered out the door," he said, "and— wham!" Then, to the relief of the Hardys, Captain Early burst into hearty laughter. Even the women had to chuckle at his predicament, and when Joe mentioned the note on the mirror, Miss Hardy confessed she had not seen it.

When the hilarity quieted down, the captain had tea with his hosts before retiring again.

The next morning at breakfast time, the doorbell rang in loud, persistent spurts.

"I'll get it," said Frank, rising from the table and hurrying to the front door.

The caller was a large, burly man with iron-gray hair. "Where's Fenton Hardy?" he demanded roughly.

"My father's not home," said Frank. "May I—"

"Get out of my way!" The man shoved him aside and started into the house.

Frank reacted angrily. "Wait a minute!" he said, grabbing the man's arm. "Just who are you and what do you want?"

The man's jaw jutted. "You'll find out—and mighty soon!"

The two might have come to blows, if the sounds of their altercation had not reached the dining room. Joe came hurrying to see what was wrong, the captain limping after him.

At sight of the Navy man, the visitor stopped short. His threatening snarl changed to a sullen scowl. For a moment there was dead silence, then the stranger muttered to Frank:

"You tell Fenton Hardy that if Gus Bock ever finds him, he's in for trouble!"

Without another word, the visitor turned and stalked out the door.

CHAPTER III

Mystery Map

BOTH the Hardys and Captain Early were too taken aback to speak for a moment.

"What the dickens was *that* all about?" Joe said finally.

"This man wanted to see Dad about something and got sore when I said he wasn't home." Frank turned to the captain. "The sight of you seemed to quiet him, sir. Do you know him?"

Captain Early shook his head slowly. "No. He did look a bit familiar, but I can't seem to place him— Wait a minute."

Suddenly the Navy man snapped his fingers. "Gus Bock! Of course! He was a bos'n third on the last destroyer I commanded. Always did have an ugly temper. Had him up before the mast many times. Believe I heard later he was court-martialed for threatening an officer."

"Any idea what he's doing now?" asked Joe.

"Hmm. Well, I know he put in for frogman training—he and another young chap who served under me on the *Svenson*. And much later I heard he was working as a commercial diver—but that was several years ago."

"Wonder what he has against Dad," Joe mused.

"Nothing serious, I hope," said Captain Early. "That fellow's a bad customer."

"Dad can take care of himself," Frank said confidently. "Let's go finish our breakfast. Sorry for the interruption, Captain."

Their aunt peered at the boys inquisitively as they returned to the table. When neither spoke, she said, "Sounded like some troublemaker. Who was he?"

Frank and Joe assumed blank, innocent expressions. Although their aunt would never admit it, she secretly followed the Hardys' mystery cases with avid interest, and both boys could see that she was consumed with curiosity over the caller.

"Just someone to see Dad," Frank said casually.

"I assumed that. I asked who he was."

"He said his name was Gus Bock."

Miss Hardy fixed Frank with a gimlet stare, then turned to Joe. The boys' eyes were twinkling. Captain Early *ahem*-ed awkwardly.

"Oh, very well. The matter's of no real concern to me." Gertrude Hardy sniffed. "But if anything serious happens as a result of that fellow's call, don't come to me later for advice or sympathy!"

The boys choked with laughter, and Frank hastened to explain all to his offended aunt. When he had finished, she commented, "Humph! So Bock is a diver. That probably means your father is on the trail of some sunken treasure, and Bock is trying to scare him off. This modern underwater craze is entirely too dangerous, anyhow. If Fenton is wise, he'll have nothing to do with the case."

With a slight smile, the boys' mother gently changed the subject. After breakfast Joe suggested to his brother that they check outside for footprints of the person they had seen in front of the window the night before. As they expected, however, the few faint traces had been all but obliterated by the rain.

"Tough luck," Frank said. "Well, at least the storm's over and the sun's out. Hey, here comes the mail!"

The postman was just ambling up the walk with his leather pouch. He greeted the boys with a cheery hello and handed over a sheaf of letters. Joe thumbed through them.

"Anything for me?" Frank asked.

"No. Just ads, mostly, and business stuff for Dad." Suddenly Joe stopped to stare at one envelope. "Say, here's a queer one— Leapin' lizards! Look at the sender's name on this, Frank!"

The older boy examined the envelope. It was

addressed to Fenton Hardy in crudely printed, red-inked letters. Far more startling was the sender's name and address in the upper left-hand corner:

R. ROGERS
WHALEBONE ISLAND

"Good night!" Frank gasped. "The same name as the pirate Captain Early told us about!"

"Whose ghost we saw at the window!" Joe added. "And don't forget, Dad wanted to know about the legend of Whalebone Island. This may tie in with the case he's working on!"

"It's postmarked Seaview," Frank noted. "That's the town on the mainland right across from the island. Come on, Joe. Let's try to raise Dad on the radio!"

The two hurried to their father's study. By luck, they were able to make short-wave contact almost at once. Fenton Hardy listened to their account of the previous night's events and exclaimed when he heard of the letter.

"Go ahead and open it, boys! This should be interesting!"

Joe slit the envelope and pulled out a rumpled, stained piece of paper. Both boys gasped when they saw what was on it.

"It's a map of Whalebone Island, Dad!" Joe reported. "No writing, except for the label—and a red X mark at one spot!"

"Any indication of what the mark stands for?"

"Not a hint. But if you want a guess, how about pirate treasure?"

"Take it easy, Joe," Frank said. "For all we know, this map may be a fake—or somebody's idea of a practical joke."

"Could be," Mr. Hardy agreed, "but I think it should be investigated—promptly. Tell me, were you two planning to go back with Captain Early to check his house for clues?"

"Yes, Dad," Joe said. "He's downstairs telephoning the garage to see when his car'll be ready."

"All right, here's a suggestion. You fellows cruise along the coast in the *Sleuth*, and then proceed on to Whalebone Island. I'll meet you there this evening."

"Swell! You've got a date, Dad!"

After signing off, the boys hurried downstairs to inform their mother. Captain Early was just hanging up the telephone.

"They have the distributor and the car will be ready in half an hour," he said.

"That's great," Frank remarked. "Joe and I will drive you to the garage and then take our motorboat to your place. We're going to meet Dad later on Whalebone Island."

The boys hastily packed some supplies and camping gear in the trunk of their convertible, amid a stream of advice and dire warnings of pirate peril from Aunt Gertrude. A short time later they drove off with Captain Early to the repair garage on the outskirts of Bayport.

"Ah, there's my car! Must be all set," said the captain, pointing to a blue sedan parked on the adjoining cinder lot.

After dropping their guest, the boys drove to the Bayport harbor. They parked and locked the convertible. Then, shouldering their camping equipment, they headed for the boathouse where the *Sleuth* was berthed.

As they neared the waterfront, a sleek, bright red motorboat came put-putting up to the pier.

"Hey, that's the *Napoli!*" Joe exclaimed. "Hi, Chet! Hi, Tony!"

Dumping their gear on the boardwalk for the moment, the Hardys hurried out to greet their two friends. Tony Prito, at the wheel of his craft, was an agile, dark-haired youth. His passenger, stowing away some tackle, was Chet Morton, chubby-faced and solidly built.

"How was the fishing?" Frank called.

Tony turned thumbs down. "Terrible!"

"We didn't catch a thing," Chet added, climbing out on the dock. "And I had my mouth all set for some nice broiled bass for lunch, too!"

"Pretty sad, pal." Joe grinned and patted the stout boy's midriff. "But think of the pounds you've saved!"

Before Chet could protest, Joe said, "Look! How would you fellows like to come with us on a search for pirate treasure?"

Tony swung eagerly up onto the pier. "You kidding?"

"See for yourself," said Joe, taking out the map.

Chet stared at it, round-eyed. "Whalebone Island! Is this really on the level?"

"The map came through the mail," Frank explained. "We don't know anything about it, but we want to find out."

Tony, whose father owned a construction business, hesitated, then shook his head. "I'd sure like to come, but my dad needs me to drive the truck."

"Well, I'm game," said Chet. "Let's hear the whole story."

"We'll tell you on the way," Joe promised.

Chet sped home to the Morton farmhouse in his jalopy to get some items of clothing and supplies. By the time he returned, the Hardys had fueled the *Sleuth* and were ready to shove off.

"Okay, now fill me in," Chet demanded as they cruised out across the calm, blue waters of Barmet Bay.

Frank scratched his head and shot a glance at Joe. "Where should we begin?"

"Let's start with us seeing the Jolly Rogers'

ghost last night," Joe suggested mischievously. "You see, Chet, he *haunts* Whalebone Island."

"H-h-haunts?" Chet paled a bit and he looked from Frank to Joe, hoping for signs of a joke. "I knew there was some catch to this. But go on."

As the story unfolded, Chet gulped and grew more nervous. His enthusiasm for the expedition seemed to be fading fast.

"Oh boy, this is just great," he complained. "Not only a ghost, but probably crooks too, if this is connected with some case your father's working on! Why is it that every time I get mixed up with you Hardys, I run smack into—"

At that moment a familiar voice crackled from the speaker of the *Sleuth's* short-wave marine radio. "Aunt Gertrude calling Frank and Joe! You must come home at once!"

CHAPTER IV

Danger Signal

FRANK seized the microphone. "*Sleuth* to Elm Street! What's wrong, Aunt Gertrude?" He added with a sudden pang of fear, "Has anything happened to Mother?"

"To Laura? Certainly not!" Miss Hardy snapped. "Your mother's right here in the house with me. In fact, she was the one who found it."

"Found what?"

"Captain Early's cane."

"Captain Early's cane?" Frank repeated, mystified. "But he took his cane with him."

"He took *a* cane with him," Miss Hardy corrected. "Your father's walking stick, to be exact—the one Fenton had to use last month when he sprained his ankle."

"You mean the captain got them switched somehow?"

"Of course. What else would I mean? Your

father slept in that room when he couldn't get up and down stairs—don't you remember? His stick was hanging on the back of a chair in there. It's that rough, knobbly brown wood, so I suppose it was easy for the captain to confuse it with his own carved cane."

"Especially with all the excitement in there last night," Frank muttered, grinning.

"What was that?"

"Er, nothing, Aunty."

Joe gave his brother an exasperated look. "Nuts! Do we have to go back, Frank? We'll lose at least an hour."

Frank thought for a moment. "No, I guess not." He spoke into the microphone. "Aunt Gertrude —the switch in canes isn't important if the captain himself didn't notice any difference. We can take the cane to him some time later or even send it."

"Humph. Well, suit yourself. At least I've informed you of his mistake."

The *Sleuth* cruised on out of Barmet Bay into the sweeping rollers of the Atlantic, then turned northward along the coast. It was nearing one o'clock when the boys finally sighted Captain Early's snug white villa perched on a bluff, amid a grove of gigantic, silvery-green poplar trees.

At the foot of the bluff was a wooden dock, to which the captain's motor cruiser was moored. As the boys brought the *Sleuth* alongside and tied up, the captain emerged from the villa and waved excitedly.

The trio scrambled onto the dock and hurried up the flight of stone steps which led from the beach to the villa.

Captain Early greeted the boys hastily and acknowledged the introduction to Chet with a quick handshake.

"By the way," Frank added, "we had a radio call from Aunt Gertrude saying you left your cane at our house and took—"

"Yes, yes, I've already discovered my mistake," Captain Early cut in. "But something more important has happened. Please come inside!"

The boys stepped into the comfortably furnished front room and saw at a glance the reason for their host's disturbance. Books had been yanked from shelves, drawers pulled out of an antique writing table, and a painting plucked down to expose a small wall safe—the door of which hung open.

"Wow!" Joe gasped.

"As you see, the place was ransacked," said Captain Early. "The study and my bedroom upstairs seem to have gotten an extra-thorough going-over."

He led the boys to the various other rooms to show them the havoc.

"Have you taken inventory yet to see what's missing?" Frank asked.

"Just a hasty one. But that's what's so strange—apparently the burglar took nothing."

"What do you keep in the house that is of value?" Joe put in.

The captain gave a perplexed shrug. "Can't think of anything, really, except the silver—and that wasn't touched. Of course there are notes and manuscripts of books that I'm working on. But they'd hardly be of value to anyone except me."

Frank said, "What about the safe?"

"Just personal papers, diaries, documents—such as my will—and two insurance policies. I had the combination jotted down in a notebook in my desk."

Joe, who had brought along the Hardys' detective kit, looked at his brother. "Let's try for some prints."

The two young sleuths dusted a number of spots in several rooms, but the only fresh prints were found to belong either to Captain Early or to Mrs. Calhoun, his part-time maid who came in on Tuesdays and Fridays.

"I'd say it's pretty obvious that the intruder wore gloves," Frank concluded.

"Well, thanks anyhow for your efforts," said the captain. "At least the fellow didn't leave me any poorer."

"This may be locking the barn after the horse is stolen, sir," said Frank, "but it might be a good idea to install a burglar alarm, or at least get a watchdog—just in case the intruder comes again."

"Hmm. Good suggestion." Captain Early nodded. "Meantime, how about some lunch?"

Chet brightened immediately. "Sure thing, sir, if you insist!"

The boys enjoyed plump lamb chops served by Mrs. Calhoun, and listened with keen interest to the captain's exciting sea yarns.

"By the way," said Captain Early as he sat back and filled his pipe, "a rather odd thing happened this morning."

"After we left you?"

"Yes. On the way home, my car ran out of gas."

Chet paused in polishing off the last morsels of lemon meringue pie. "That's happened to my jalopy three times. I found out my gas gauge was stuck."

"Well, there's nothing wrong with *my* gauge," said the captain. "The needle showed empty. But it happens that I filled up yesterday, so there should have been quite a bit of gasoline still left in the tank."

"Sure your tank wasn't leaking?" Joe inquired.

"Positive. I checked that later."

The Hardys exchanged puzzled glances. Their father had taught them to disregard no possible clue, however slight, when working on a mystery.

"What happened, sir?" said Frank. "I mean after you ran out of gas."

"Oh, no trouble, luckily. I was picked up almost immediately by a motorist who gave me a lift to the next gas station. Then one of the station hands drove me back in a tow truck with a can of gas."

Frank's forehead creased thoughtfully. "If the garage mechanic parked your car on the outside lot overnight, someone could have drained most of the gas."

"Why should anyone do that?"

"I don't know. But it might have been done to give someone a chance to get at your car after you stalled and left it parked along the highway."

Joe objected. "That doesn't add up. If someone was able to drain the tank during the night, he could have got at the car right then and there."

"Maybe he did, but couldn't find what he was after," Frank argued. "Captain, when you went for gas, did you leave anything in the car that wasn't in it last night?"

Captain Early shook his head. "No, nor can I think of anything valuable that I'd be likely to leave in the car at any time."

Another mystery—and again the Hardy boys had to confess they were baffled. However, Frank and Joe promised to continue work on the case after they returned from Whalebone Island.

Captain Early stumped down the stone stairs to the dock with the three Bayporters and waved good-by as the *Sleuth* headed on up the coast.

It was late in the afternoon when they finally reached the town of Seaview. The boys put in to a commercial dock to replenish their fuel, then turned seaward toward Whalebone Island, which lay about twenty miles offshore.

Dusk settled over the ocean and a few stars came out.

Presently the vague mass of Whalebone Island loomed ahead through the darkness. The tower of its old stone lighthouse stood out against the velvety purple sky.

"Where do we land?" Chet inquired.

"Dad said there's a little natural cove or harbor around on the southern side," Joe replied. "He's going to meet us there on the beach."

Suddenly a red glow flashed from the lighthouse tower. It disappeared—to be followed by two shorter blinks, then others. The boys were startled.

"That's no ordinary light!" said Chet. "Red means danger!"

"It's a code signal," Frank murmured. He spelled out the letters of the message as they were flashed in Morse blinker:

D-A-N-G-E-R! K-E-E-P A-W-A-Y H-A-R-D-Y-S!

CHAPTER V

The Golden Pharaoh

AWESTRUCK by the weird red-light signals, the boys sat hunched in their seats as the *Sleuth* plowed onward through the darkness toward Whalebone Island. Joe was the first to break their stunned silence.

"I don't get it. Was that meant as a warning for us to stay away from the island—or an order to someone to *keep* us away?"

"What's the difference?" moaned Chet. "Either way, we're asking for trouble if we go ahead and land at that spooky place!"

Joe—who knew his friend's sterling qualities could be depended upon in a tight spot—reached out and gave Chet a reassuring whack. "Relax, Strongheart!" Joe chuckled. "A spook wouldn't stand a chance against a beefy bruiser like you!"

"Oh, no? Well, I still vote we head back to the mainland."

"Take it easy," Frank said soothingly. "Remember, Dad will be on the island to meet us."

The Hardys knew, from the mystery map and their chart, that Whalebone Island was shaped like a crescent. It curved from southwest to northeast, with the outward bulge to the north. Frank steered for the southern horn of the crescent. As the splash of breakers told him they were nearing land, he cut the engine and allowed the *Sleuth* to drift the rest of the way to shore.

An eerie silence lay over the island. It was broken only by the faint sighing of the night breeze and the sounds of the surf. When they had reached the shallows, Joe kicked off his sneakers and climbed over the side to help beach the boat among some reeds.

When they were safely ashore, Chet said, "Now what?"

"We'll cut across the tip of the island to the cove," Frank said, "and meet Dad."

The boys made their way over a ridge of dunes, topped by scrub. On the other side lay the inward curve of the crescent, indented by a sheltered cove near the center. A small blaze flickered on the beach.

"Dad's campfire!" Joe exclaimed.

The boys hurried along the shore, but as they came closer, they could see no one at the fire. Vaguely alarmed, they broke into a sprint, forgetting all caution.

Reaching the campfire, they saw that a stoutly built boat with an outboard motor had been drawn up on the sand. Near the fire lay a sleeping bag, supplies, cooking utensils, and a short-wave transceiver.

"That's Dad's radio!" said Frank.

The boys stared about through the darkness. If Mr. Hardy was concealed among the scattered trees and brush, he gave no sign of his presence. Joe gave the Hardys' special whistle, and repeated it several times, but there was no reply.

"Hey! Maybe he saw those signals and went to the lighthouse to investigate," Joe said in a hushed voice.

"Perhaps he sent the signals himself to warn us away," Chet conjectured.

"Could be," said Frank. "We'd better go there and take a look."

The brothers had brought powerful flashlights, but used them as little as possible in making their way across the island. The terrain was humped with low hills, fringed with patches of stunted oak and pine. At the northern horn of the crescent, the land rose to a rocky eminence topped by the Whalebone Light.

Cautiously the trio approached the forbidding stone tower, trying to keep their feet from scrunching on the grit and gravel. Frank tried the door, then pushed it open. Something blocked it partway—an obstruction that yielded slightly as he shoved harder.

Frank inserted his head and right shoulder into the opening and switched on his flashlight. "Dad!" he cried out.

Joe squeezed in behind his brother, and Chet followed. The beam of Frank's flashlight revealed the figure of Mr. Hardy sprawled on the concrete floor. A thin trickle of red from his scalp had clotted across the left temple.

"Somebody knocked him out!" Frank said worriedly.

The three squatted down anxiously and Frank checked his father's pulse. It was beating strongly. Joe hurried outside, scrambled down to the water's edge, and returned a few moments later with his handkerchief soaked with cold brine. After the boys had applied it to their father's forehead and chafed his wrists, Mr. Hardy began to revive.

"Joe— Frank— Hi, Chet." The detective gave them a rueful smile, then slowly raised himself to a sitting position.

"What happened, Dad?" asked Frank.

Mr. Hardy frowned and rubbed his hand over his eyes. "Let me see— Oh, yes, those red-light signals from the tower here."

"We saw 'em too!" declared Chet.

"So did I—from my campsite on the other side

"Somebody knocked out Dad!" Frank said worriedly

of the island," Mr. Hardy went on slowly. "I came over to investigate, entered this doorway, and—wham!"

"How do you feel now?" Joe inquired.

"Not too bad, except for this throbbing lump. Lucky for me I have a thick skull."

The boys helped Fenton Hardy to his feet, then began a search of the tower. They checked every floor, up to the lantern room, but the assailant had vanished. Warily, the detective and the three youths tramped back across the island to his camp on the cove.

The fire had long since burned down to glowing embers. After it had been replenished with driftwood and dry brush, Frank showed his father the cablegram from Egypt and the map which had been sent through the mail by "R. Rogers."

"What's this Pharaoh's head you're supposed to beware of, Dad?" asked Joe.

"It's a solid gold bust of the Egyptian Pharaoh, or Emperor, Rhamaton IV—valued at one million dollars."

Chet let out an awed whistle. "A *million bucks!* Wow! Where is this head, Mr. Hardy?"

"A good question, Chet," the detective replied wryly. "I'd better start at the beginning. About two weeks ago, a freighter named the *Katawa* sank off the coast. Maybe you fellows recall hearing about it in the news. Several of the crew, including the purser, drowned."

"It was rammed in a fog by some cruise liner, wasn't it?" said Frank.

"That's right—by the *Carona*. Well, the spot where the freighter went down is just a couple of miles north of Whalebone Island."

Mr. Hardy explained that the *Katawa* had been carrying not only cargo, but also a dozen passengers—one of them a foreign art dealer named Zufar, who had boarded the ship at Beirut in the Middle East.

"Zufar was bringing the golden Pharaoh's head with him," the detective continued, "to sell to a customer in New York. And the head was allegedly in the ship's strong room when the *Katawa* sank. Zufar has lodged a claim with Transmarine Underwriters, the line's insurance company, for a million dollars."

"The news stories on the sinking never mentioned the Pharaoh's head, did they?" Joe asked.

"No. As a security precaution, Zufar had purposely avoided any publicity about the treasure, and since the sinking, the line has also tried to keep the matter out of the news for the same reason."

"You said the head was *allegedly* in the ship's strong room," said Frank. "Is there some doubt about it?"

"That's where the mystery comes in, and that's why Transmarine has engaged me to investigate the case," Mr. Hardy replied. "They've been tipped off that a gold head of Rhamaton IV is secretly being offered for sale."

"Was the tip on the level?" Joe asked.

"So far we don't know. I've been checking it out, but may not know the answer until divers get at the *Katawa's* strong room. Meantime, the tip brings up a number of interesting possibilities."

"Right," Frank said. "The head being offered for sale might be a fake. Either that, or the one that went down with the *Katawa* was a phony."

Mr. Hardy smiled at the rapid-fire deductions, as Joe added, "Maybe the treasure already has been salvaged from the sunken hulk."

Chet joined in. "Hey! The head might not have been on the ship at all!"

"Exactly," said Mr. Hardy. "It may have been filched from the *Katawa* back in Beirut—or even in Le Havre, France, where she stopped before the crossing to New York."

Frank grinned and inquired, "How come you were so interested in the legend of Whalebone Island, Dad?"

"Because I have a feeling it may tie in with this case." Fenton Hardy stirred up the fire, adding, "Before we do any more talking, let's have another look at that map."

Joe handed him the paper.

"Hmm. The X mark appears to lie between two hills directly back of this cove," said the detective.

Frank bent close to peer at the map. "And these trees form a sort of arrowhead triangle pointing right at the spot."

Mr. Hardy rubbed his jaw. "I'm wondering if we should investigate now or wait until morning. I'd feel a lot better knowing who knocked me out —and just where he's lurking."

"If you ask me, that's a good reason for checking out the X mark right now," said Joe. "Suppose something valuable is stashed there, Dad. The person who conked you may be after it—and he might just snatch it during the night."

"You have a point there, son," the detective conceded. "Very well. If you're all willing, let's go look."

Dousing their campfire, the group headed inland. Beyond the screen of trees sheltering the cove, the ground rose slightly, then flattened again amid a tangle of brush that made their going difficult in the darkness.

Presently Frank halted and touched his father's arm. "Look! Those must be the three trees, Dad!"

His beam, moving back and forth, showed three scrubby trees, positioned like the points of a triangle.

Mr. Hardy nodded. "No doubt about it. Those humps on the skyline up ahead are two shallow hills."

The four advanced cautiously past the trees. In

a few moments they came to the brink of a steep ravine, cupped between the hills.

They began clambering down the slope into the gully. Joe shifted his flashlight to his left hand in order to seize hold of some underbrush and steady his descent. As the yellow beam veered toward the left bank of the ravine, he let out a sudden startled yell.

"Look! There's somebody!"

The others turned hastily, but the figure had darted out of sight.

"Where did he go?" Mr. Hardy asked.

"Among that shrubbery. I didn't get a good look, but he—"

Joe's words were drowned out by a terrific blast! The left wall of the ravine exploded with a shattering force!

CHAPTER VI

A Madman's Scrawl

THE blast knocked the sleuths flat against the bank of the ravine as fragments of rock and earth showered down upon them.

"Are you all right, boys?" gasped Fenton Hardy.

Three voices reassured him. Frank lay on his flashlight, and when he pulled it free, the beam still shone. Joe's light had been buried somewhere in the debris.

"Whew!" Chet gulped as he struggled upright. "Feels like I just got creamed by a whole football line!"

"Let's get out of here," Mr. Hardy said.

Shaking the dust from their clothes, the four clambered back up to level ground. Frank turned and shone his beam down into the ravine, the bottom of which was heaped with rubble.

"That fellow you saw, Joe—what did he look like?"

"I hardly had time to see his face at all," Joe replied, "but two things I did notice were—a red beard and a black cloak!"

Chet groaned. "The Jolly Roger ghost again!"

"I doubt if ghosts are capable of planting explosives," Mr. Hardy said dryly. "It was probably the same person who hit me."

"Think we should try to hunt him down, Dad?" asked Frank, aiming his flashlight beam toward the brush-covered hillside left of the ravine.

"No. We wouldn't stand a chance of finding him in this darkness. Worse yet, we'd make easy targets. Better switch your light off, son."

"For that matter, we'd be sitting ducks around a campfire," Joe reasoned.

"True enough—which is why we're not going to risk it," said Mr. Hardy. "Our safest bet is to hole up in the lighthouse until morning. After that, we can decide our next move."

Under cover of the darkness, the group made their way slowly northeast toward the Whalebone Lighthouse, using the dim outline of the tower as a direction guide.

Not until they reached the lighthouse did Joe realize that one of their party was missing.

"Hey! Where's Chet?" he exclaimed, wheeling about.

All three Hardys peered back anxiously the way

they had come. The glow of the misty half-moon, low in the sky, revealed no sign of Chet.

They exchanged glances of dismay. Had somebody bushwhacked Chet?

"Joe and I'll go back and find him," Frank said.

"Not without me," their father replied.

Stealthy as Indians the trio began to retrace their steps. Frank and Joe moved along cautiously at their father's side—sick with fear that at any moment they might discover their pal's motionless body.

They had just reached a dense thicket of shrubbery near the ravine when a crackling noise caused them to halt abruptly.

"Hit the ground!" Mr. Hardy murmured. Silently the three sleuths flattened themselves in the brush.

The noise came closer and the form of a man materialized out of the gloom. Without hesitation, Joe hurled himself through the darkness. There was a grunt of impact, and as he butted against solid flesh, Joe felt a heavy stick swish past his ear and whack him hard on the shoulder. He went down in a tangle of arms and legs just as Frank snapped on a flashlight.

"Hey, what's the big idea! You guys trying to ambush me or something?"

"Chet!" Frank gasped.

Grinning ruefully, Joe got up while Frank

helped Chet to his feet. Mr. Hardy was already retrieving several cans, a squashed loaf of bread, and other supplies which lay scattered over the ground.

"Where the dickens have *you* been, Chet?—as if we couldn't guess," Frank said.

"And what's the idea of trying to brain me with that stick?" Joe added.

"You think I'd be dopey enough to let that red-whiskered nut jump me, without being set for him?" Chet retorted.

Mr. Hardy found it difficult to restrain a smile. "Good for you, Chet—but you did have us pretty badly worried, disappearing like that without a word of explanation."

Chet gulped. "I was afraid you wouldn't let me if I asked to go back for grub. But—well, gosh, how could we get through the whole night without something to eat? I haven't had a thing since lunch."

Joe chuckled. "You put away enough lamb chops at Captain Early's to hold you for a week!"

"Oh, yeah? I only had four of those little bitty things."

"All the same," said Mr. Hardy, putting on a straight face, "it was a foolish risk going back to the campfire after what happened."

"Oh, I didn't go back *there*," Chet explained. "I got this stuff off the *Sleuth*."

"Okay, I guess we can all use some food," Frank said. "Now let's make tracks for the lighthouse."

Although the Whalebone Light had been abandoned years before, the keeper's living quarters still contained various furnishings—a battered table and chairs, a cast-iron stove, and a glass-chimneyed kerosene lamp. The storeroom below contained two rusty lanterns and several tins of oil and kerosene, evidently left behind for the use of stranded fishermen.

With the tower door securely barred behind them, the group soon cooked a tasty supper and fell to with keen appetites. Afterward, they sat around the table talking.

"Can you tell us more, Dad, of why you were interested in the legend of Whalebone Island?" said Frank.

"A good detective," Mr. Hardy replied, "should always be concerned when something odd happens at or near the scene of a case he's investigating."

"You mean, something strange went on here before tonight?" Joe asked.

"Yes. Several days ago I saw an item in the newspaper about a fisherman who'd reported being scared out of his wits by the ghost of Whalebone Island when he put in one evening."

Frank said, "So you suspected that something funny might be going on here."

"Exactly. It seemed far more likely that the so-called 'ghost' might be someone who was using the circumstances of the legend as a cover-up for some secret activity—and also, of course, to scare people away from the island."

"What kind of secret stuff?" Chet asked.

"Somebody might be using the island as a base for diving operations to the *Katawa*."

"Which would explain why the golden Pharaoh's head was secretly being offered for sale!" Joe declared.

"Not only that," said Mr. Hardy. "The *Katawa*'s hulk is vitally important for another reason. You see, there's a fortune in lawsuits at stake over the losses and injuries suffered in the collision, particularly claims being brought by relatives of those who lost their lives."

"But how does that make the sunken hulk so important?" Joe questioned.

"The *Katawa*'s master claims his ship was stopped dead in the water after they picked up an approaching vessel on radar. If he's right, Transmarine is free and clear of responsibility. But the captain of the *Carona* alleges that the *Katawa* was proceeding at full speed in spite of the fog—in which case Transmarine could be liable for several million dollars in damages, not even counting the loss of the gold Pharaoh's head."

"And the answer lies aboard the sunken freighter?" put in Frank.

"Right—with the engine-room telegraph and tachometer," Mr. Hardy answered. "If the telegraph shows 'Stop' and the tachometer reads 'Zero,' the *Katawa* was not at fault. If they indicate full speed ahead, it's a different story—a difference worth several million dollars."

Joe gave a low whistle. "Some difference!"

Suddenly Frank snapped his fingers. "That mention of diving reminds me, Dad—in all the excitement about the pirate map, we clean forgot to tell you about the visitor you had this morning!" He quickly described Gus Bock's appearance at the Hardy home and the threat which the diver had uttered before leaving.

Mr. Hardy took the news calmly. "I think I have the answer to that." He explained that Transmarine Underwriters had asked him to run a security check on several competing diving companies before letting the contract to salvage the *Katawa.*

"Gus Bock," the sleuth went on, "is chief diver for an outfit called the Simon Salvage Company. They tried hard to get the contract, even put in a ridiculously low bid. But the company has a shady reputation. They've been involved in outright fights and several other unsavory incidents on salvage jobs, so I advised against them."

Instead, Mr. Hardy told the boys, he had recommended that the contract go to the Crux Diving Company. As a result, Gus Bock was no doubt out for revenge.

"How about what happened tonight?" Chet said, looking around the table uneasily. "Do you think Bock or Simon Salvage was behind that explosion in the ravine?"

"It's a cinch the map was just bait to lure us there," Joe declared.

"I agree," said Fenton Hardy. "The real question is who sent it—and who has been posing as Red Rogers' ghost."

"What's our next move, Dad?" Frank asked.

"Come daylight, we'll search the island for clues to the person who tried to kill us. After that, we'd all better return to the mainland. I have to get back to work with Sam Radley, tracing that tip on the Pharaoh's head."

Next morning, while Chet Morton and Mr. Hardy were preparing breakfast, Frank and Joe started up the winding stairway of the tower to check the lamp room for possible traces of the person who had sent the red warning signals.

As they neared the top, Frank suddenly halted and pointed to the wall. "Take a look at that, Joe!"

A message—faded and almost illegible—had been scrawled in pencil on the whitewashed surface of the stone. It said:

I've seen Rogers again. No mistake this time. He's come back and he's trying to drive me out of my mind. Heaven help me!

R. H. Tang 4/17/45

CHAPTER VII

The Midnight Wrecker

"TANG!" Joe gasped. "The lighthouse keeper who went out of his mind!"

"I wonder," Frank said slowly, "if he *was* suffering from hallucinations."

Joe stared at his brother. "Are you implying that Tang *wasn't* crazy?"

"Suppose we told a doctor we'd seen the Jolly Roger ghost—a red-bearded spook in a black cloak. And not just here on Whalebone Island, but even back in Bayport. Would he call *us* crazy?"

"The explosion last night wasn't our imagination!" Joe said flatly.

"Maybe. But that wouldn't prove we had or hadn't seen a ghost."

"Still," Joe persisted, "Tang must have been examined before he could be declared insane."

"True, but the question is what really drove him out of his mind?" Frank argued. "Suppose you or I were cooped up in this tower alone for

weeks and months, not another soul on the island
—so far as we knew. Yet every time we went for a
walk to stretch our legs, that spook kept popping
out at us—especially at night. Maybe even inside
the lighthouse. I'll bet we'd be flipping our wigs
too before long!"

Joe frowned reflectively, then blurted out,
"But, good night, Frank! All that was years ago.
The person Tang saw couldn't have been the
same one *we* saw—"

As Joe's voice trailed off, Frank gave a wry
chuckle. "You mean—or could it? That's the same
question I'm asking myself."

The lamp room had been empty ever since the
Whalebone Light was taken out of service. The
boys inspected it thoroughly, but found no clues to
the signaler.

"He must have used an ordinary bull's-eye lantern. Let's try the outside platform and see if—"
Joe broke off with a gasp. "Hey, Frank!"

"What's the matter?"

"Look there—out to sea!"

Lying off the southern shore of the island was a
small steamer. Larger than a tug, it was equipped
with cargo booms.

The two boys dashed to the floor below and
outside to the railed platform around the light
tower.

"It's not under way," Joe observed. "What do
you think it's doing out there?"

"Could be a fishing vessel," Frank said doubtfully, "but it sure doesn't look like one. Let's get Dad."

On hearing the news, Mr. Hardy and Chet hurried topside. The detective broke out his powerful binoculars and focused on the mysterious vessel.

"It's a salvage ship!" Mr. Hardy said tensely. "It belongs to the Simon Salvage Company."

"Gus Bock's outfit!" exclaimed Joe.

Mr. Hardy passed the binoculars to the boys. Each of the three in turn examined the vessel. The name at its stern read:

SIMON SALVOR
NEW YORK

On deck, a diver had apparently just suited up. Helpers were closing the glass ports of his helmet and checking the air hose and telephone cable. As Frank watched, the diver strode to the side of the ship and climbed down a ladder into the water.

"That must be Bock himself," Frank muttered. "But what's he diving for there, Dad? You said the *Katawa* went down *north* of the island, didn't you?"

Mr. Hardy frowned. "That's right. And I can't figure Simon Salvage engaging in a diving operation just for the fun of it."

"I wonder when the ship arrived," Joe mused. "We didn't see it last night."

"Maybe it was on the other side of the island," put in Chet. Suddenly a look of comprehension crossed his face. "Oh—oh! You think maybe somebody off that ship was the dynamiter last night?"

"Sure, and also the one who flashed those red signals," Joe replied.

"It's possible, all right," Mr. Hardy agreed.

"Dad, I have an idea!" Frank exclaimed.

"Let's hear it, son."

"When you go back to the mainland, why don't we three stay on the island? We can watch the *Simon Salvor* and maybe find out what it's up to— and also keep a lookout for the 'ghost'!"

Mr. Hardy looked troubled. He shook his head. "That would be dangerous, Frank. There's no telling what might happen with a possible killer at large."

Frank and Joe pleaded earnestly. Mr. Hardy finally promised to wait until they searched the island before making a final decision.

After breakfast they scoured the Whalebone crescent from tip to tip, but the ghostly dynamiter had apparently slipped away during the night. The detective was now half inclined to let the boys stay.

When they approached the cove campsite at the end of their search, Fenton Hardy stopped short and blanched.

"My camp's been ransacked!"

The four rushed forward. Scattered across the

sand were the smashed fragments of what had been his transceiver.

"Who—" Joe began, appalled. The sleeping bag was burned to a charred crisp. All food supplies were violently trampled.

The detective's boat, too, seemed to be gone. But suddenly Frank's sharp eyes spotted the craft.

"There it is!" he said, pointing offshore.

The boat lay bottom-up in a few feet of water, a gaping hole in its hull!

Fenton Hardy's jaw tightened grimly. "That settles it," he said. "You boys are not staying on the island. We're going back in the *Sleuth* together—if our ghost hasn't wrecked that, too."

Anxiously they trekked back to the southern tip of the island. All four heaved sighs of relief when they found the sleek motorboat still safely hidden among the reeds.

Before leaving, they cruised back to the cove to salvage the outboard motor from Mr. Hardy's stove-in craft. Chet, using the binoculars, saw a man on the bridge of the *Simon Salvor* watching them intently through a telescope.

Later, as the *Sleuth* put-putted out of the cove, the *Salvor* moved away from shore. "Not taking any chances on us coming out to snoop," Joe observed.

The Bayporters headed to the mainland at a fast clip.

Ashore, Mr. Hardy reported the loss of his rented craft to the boat livery and returned the water-logged outboard engine.

The owner took the news philosophically. "Don't matter too much—she was insured," he said. "Have to hold your deposit, though, till I settle with the insurance company."

The detective nodded, then asked, "By the way, you wouldn't happen to know if any boat put in here during the night—or maybe early this morning?"

"You figure that mighta been the party who scuttled *your* boat?" The liveryman squinted shrewdly at Mr. Hardy. "So happens I did hear o' one comin' back last night. Try Lawson's Livery down the wharf a ways—it's the only other boat rental place in town."

Mr. Hardy thanked him, then strode along the wharf with the three boys. At the other boat livery, the investigator repeated his question to the proprietor, Eli Lawson.

"Sure, there was a boat come in," Lawson said grumpily. "Must've been sometime between midnight and four o'clock. It was a boat that'd been stolen from me the night before."

"Stolen!" Mr. Hardy exclaimed.

Frank and Joe looked at each other excitedly.

More than likely, the boat thief had been the island ghost!

"How come you're so interested?" Lawson asked the detective.

Mr. Hardy told briefly how his rented boat had been sabotaged on Whalebone Island, but said nothing about the rest of the night's events.

"Say! By any chance, is your name Fenton Hardy?" the proprietor inquired.

"That's right. Why?"

Lawson went into the boathouse and emerged a moment later holding a soiled envelope. "When I found the boat this mornin', this was lyin' on one o' the seats."

The envelope bore the name "Fenton Hardy" lettered in pencil. The detective opened it and took out the enclosed note. His face hardened as he read. Then he handed the message to the boys. It said:

> *Keep away from Whalebone Island. Next time you won't escape.*

Instead of a signature there was the crude drawing of an Egyptian-looking head surmounted by a Pharaoh's headdress.

"The Pharaoh's head!" Chet gulped.

Frank and Joe silenced him with warning looks, and Mr. Hardy thanked the liveryman. The four walked away under Lawson's inquisitive gaze.

"Is that what the golden head of Rhamaton looks like, Dad?" Frank inquired when they were out of earshot.

"Yes, almost exactly. I've seen a photograph of it."

The boys accompanied Mr. Hardy to the parking lot where he had left his car overnight. It was decided that Frank and Joe would return to Bayport with Chet and wait for the arrival of Sam Radley.

"I'll send Sam back from Philadelphia as soon as I can spare him," the investigator promised. "Then he can go to Whalebone Island with you."

"Right, Dad!"

Mr. Hardy climbed into his car and sped off in the direction of the turnpike. Frank, Joe, and Chet embarked in the *Sleuth* and were soon cruising down the coast toward Barmet Bay.

It was late in the day when the Hardy boys arrived home. Aunt Gertrude's face was anxious as she greeted them.

"Well! Thank goodness you're home at last! Why didn't you answer my radio call last night?"

"Sorry, Aunty," Frank apologized. "We were away from the *Sleuth* most of the time."

"Anything wrong?" Joe asked.

"Indeed there was! Someone tried to break into the house!"

CHAPTER VIII

Egyptian Fake

An attempted break-in while they were gone! Startled, Frank and Joe wondered what the thief had been after.

"Tell us about it, Aunt Gertrude!" Frank said.

"Well, to begin with, I was all alone in the house—"

"Alone! What about Mother?" Joe broke in.

"She was called away yesterday afternoon," Miss Hardy explained, "to stay with a sick friend over in Bartonsville, Mrs. Filer. Gloria Filer, that is— Laura's old schoolmate. Well, I was sound asleep and suddenly the burglar alarm went off full blast!"

The boys' aunt shuddered at the recollection. "Heavens! It must have wakened the whole neighborhood—that shrill racket and all the floodlights blazing on!"

"Did you get a look at whoever touched it off?" Frank asked.

"No, I rushed to stick my head out the window, but the rascal was nowhere in sight. Probably ran off the instant the lights went on."

Miss Hardy eyed her nephews severely. "I tried at once to contact you two or Fenton on the radio, but got no answer."

"We were holed up in a lighthouse with a spook after us," Joe explained.

"Humph." His aunt gave him a suspicious glare through her spectacles. "Be that as it may, I was here alone—helpless. I might have been murdered in my sleep!"

The boys managed to mollify her by complimenting her on her courage and presence of mind.

"Did you call the police, Aunty?" Frank asked.

"Naturally. But they found no footprints, no clues of any kind."

Suddenly she again looked annoyed. "Which reminds me. The curator called from the new Howard Museum."

"Mr. Scath?" said Frank, immediately interested. "What did he want?"

"Wouldn't tell me. Just asked to speak to Fenton or one of you." Miss Hardy sniffed. "I suppose he thought not being in the detective business I wasn't bright enough to take a message."

"I doubt that, Aunt Gertrude." Grinning,

Frank went to the phone and called the Howard Museum. In a few moments he reached Mr. Scath.

"Glad you called, Frank," the curator said. "Something rather odd has come up. Since your father serves as our security adviser, I thought I'd better pass the word along."

"What's it about, sir?"

Mr. Scath explained that he had received a telephone call just before lunch. "The man wouldn't give his name, but he warned me that someone might contact the museum soon and try to sell me a fake Egyptian art object."

Frank's eyebrows shot up. "Did he say who this phony was, or what the object would be?"

"No hint at all. In fact, he hung up before I could ask any questions."

"Thanks for letting us know, Mr. Scath," said Frank. "Dad's out of town right now, but that tip could be very important. If any such art faker does show up, I'd appreciate it if you'd let us know right away."

"I'll certainly do that."

After completing the call, Frank told his brother the news.

"Wow! A fake *Egyptian* art object!" Joe exclaimed. "It could be an imitation of the Pharaoh's head Dad's looking for."

"Just what I was thinking," Frank said.

The Hardy boys decided to sleep downstairs,

in case the unknown prowler might make another attempt to break into the house. But the night passed without incident.

The next morning the two boys decided to go to the beach for a swim.

"Let's stop off at Chet's and see if he wants to come," Joe suggested.

Under a blaze of dazzling sunshine they started off in their convertible. Presently they turned up a dirt lane that led to the Morton farmhouse, just outside of Bayport. Two girls were seated on the front porch.

Iola, Chet's pixie-faced, dark-haired sister, was Joe's favorite date. She hopped up from the porch swing to greet the visitors. "Hi, you two ghost hunters!"

Her friend, Callie Shaw, a pretty brown-eyed blond girl, chimed in, "What's the latest on the Whalebone spook?"

"Last we heard, he needed a shave," said Frank, climbing out of the car and smiling at Callie, whom he liked very much.

"Where's Strongheart?" Joe asked.

At that moment Chet burst out through the screen door, munching on a large Danish pastry.

"Somebody call me? Oh, hi, fellows!"

"What's that—breakfast or lunch?" Frank asked with a grin.

Iola laughed. "With Chet, there's no hard and fast distinction."

"Aw, cut it out," the chubby youth said good-naturedly. "I'm just finishing breakfast." He added to the Hardys, "Slept late, that's all. Who wouldn't after that rugged expedition you guys roped me into!"

"Okay, you're excused," Frank said. "But get your trunks. We're going to the beach."

"You girls like to come?" Joe asked casually.

"We'd love to, but how can we?" said Callie. "We have to put our hair up for the party."

"What party?" Frank asked.

"What party! This afternoon, at Biff Hooper's. Don't tell me you forgot!"

The Hardys exchanged blank looks, then recalled Biff's word-of-mouth invitation during a sandlot baseball game last Monday afternoon.

The Hoopers were leaving Friday on a two-week vacation trip to California, so Biff had decided to have a going-away party on Thursday. The affair was to be an early barbecue supper, since he and his parents had to pack and prepare for a seven-o'clock take-off the next morning.

"I guess we did forget," Joe admitted. "We've been sort of busy."

"Sure, sure, we know," Iola said, dimpling. "Incidentally, Biff told us yesterday he has a surprise announcement to make at the party."

"Announcement about what?"

Iola threw up her hands. "Don't ask us. It all

sounded very mysterious. Maybe he was just trying to whet our curiosity."

"Just as long as he doesn't whet Chet's appetite," Joe needled.

Everyone laughed and Chet went back into the
house to get his swim trunks.

The Hardys could hear the sound of a telephone ringing. A few moments later, as they were
chatting with the girls, Mrs. Morton put her head
out the back door.

"Frank and Joe—"

"Yes, Mrs. Morton?"

"Your aunt just phoned. She asked me to tell
you that Mr. Scath from the museum called again
—some man is on his way to the house to see
you."

The boys jumped to their feet. "Did Aunt Gertrude say who he was?" Frank asked.

"No, but I guess it must be urgent. She advised
you both to come home at once."

As they were thanking Chet's mother for the
information, Chet returned, holding a rolled
towel under one arm. "What's the matter?" he inquired plaintively. "Is the swim off?"

"Maybe not," said Frank. "Come on back to the
house with us. We can whip over to the beach as
soon as Joe and I talk to this visitor, whoever he
is."

The three boys climbed into the convertible
and sped back to the Hardy home at High and Elm

streets, where they hurried into the kitchen.

"What's up, Aunty?" Joe inquired. "Did Mr. Scath tell you who's coming to see us—or why?"

Miss Hardy looked up from the pie dough she was rolling and pursed her lips. "He didn't, and I'm sure I have no idea of the reason for his visit, since none of you has seen fit to take me into your confidence about this mystery."

The boys' grins faded as the front doorbell rang. Frank and Joe hurried to answer it.

The caller was a fat, balding, dark-complexioned man in a white silk suit. "Is this the Hardy residence?" he asked.

"Yes. Please come in," Frank said.

The man stepped inside and handed the boys an ornate visiting card, which read:

Mehmet Zufar
Dealer in Middle Eastern
Antiquities and Objets d' Art

Cairo, Egypt

Frank and Joe glanced at the card, then looked at each other excitedly. *Their visitor was the owner of the golden Pharaoh's head!*

CHAPTER IX

The Shattered Cat

"I SHOULD like to see Mr. Fenton Hardy, the detective," said the stout visitor.

Joe found himself staring with fascination at the man's tiny black mustache, which twirled upward at each end.

"Our father's out of town just now, working on a case," Frank explained. "If you'll have a chair and tell us why you came, perhaps we can help."

Mehmet Zufar glared irritably, but nonetheless seated himself in the living room. Plucking out a handkerchief, he dabbed the beads of perspiration from his large forehead.

"My dear young man," Zufar snapped, "Fenton Hardy was recommended to me as the ablest private investigator in America. In fact, I was referred to him on a matter of the utmost importance by Mr. Scath, the museum curator. I did not come to deal with boys!"

Frank said evenly, "I just thought we might help."

"If you'll tell us what you want," Joe put in, "we'll inform Dad as soon as we can get in touch with him."

Zufar glared for a moment, then said abruptly, "My card, please!"

The art dealer fished a gold pencil from an inside pocket and jotted something on the back of the card. "When Mr. Hardy is free," he said, "please have him contact me at this address in New York."

With a final swipe of his handkerchief, Zufar clapped his straw hat back on his glistening dome and rose to depart.

"May we call you a taxi?" Frank offered.

"No, thank you. My car is outside." The stout man stalked off without another word.

As the door closed behind him, Frank and Joe dashed to the front window for a better view. They saw Zufar climb into a black limousine. A hulking, granite-faced chauffeur slammed the car door, returned to the wheel, and drove off.

"Who was that sourpuss?" inquired Chet, coming up behind the Hardys.

"The owner of the golden Pharaoh," Joe replied. "I'd sure like to know what he was so worked up about—he wouldn't tell us."

"Maybe Mr. Scath can give us the lowdown." Frank glanced at his watch. "Come on! We can stop off at the museum on our way to the beach!"

Ten minutes later the Hardys' convertible turned into the curving driveway of the Howard Museum, which stood well back from the street among landscaped grounds. The three boys hurried up the broad marble steps of the ivy-clad building and went straight to the curator's office.

Mr. Scath, a slender man with wispy strands of hair and rimless pince-nez, rose to greet his visitors as they entered.

"Come in, boys, and sit down. I take it you've just talked to Mr. Zufar."

"That's right, sir," said Frank. "But he insisted on seeing Dad and wouldn't tell us what he wanted. We hoped you might fill us in."

"Hmm, yes. Well, he came here this morning and introduced himself as an art dealer specializing in Middle Eastern antiquities. Then he tried to interest me in a blue faience Egyptian cat, dating back to the Twentieth Dynasty."

"Faience?" Joe repeated. "What's that?"

"Earthenware, coated with an opaque glaze."

Frank then asked the curator, "Did you tell Mr. Zufar about the warning you received—that someone would try to sell you an Egyptian fake?"

"Indeed, I did. I told him so bluntly." Mr. Scath gave a shrug of distaste. "The result was quite upsetting."

"What happened?" Frank asked.

"Zufar became very emotional. He said that some enemy—he didn't know who—was trying to ruin his reputation."

"Meaning," Joe guessed, "the anonymous tip you received?"

"Yes. And he said someone had evidently spread a similar rumor about a much more valuable object which he had hoped to bring to this country."

Frank bent forward eagerly. "Did he mention what the object was?"

"Not then," Mr. Scath replied, "But he did later—a solid gold head of the Pharaoh Rhamaton IV, valued at one million dollars."

Chet's eyes bulged.

The curator went on, "However, as I say, that came later. At the moment he was too worked up trying to convince me of his spotless reputation." Mr. Scath sighed. "Anyway, Zufar gave me various personal references to call and urged me to inspect the faience cat as carefully as I pleased."

"What did you do?" Joe asked.

Mr. Scath looked uncomfortable. "I didn't quite know what to do. Finally I called two of the references he gave me—another museum and a private collector. They both assured me that their dealings with Zufar had been entirely satisfactory. They both felt he was too keen to be taken in by a fake and wouldn't risk trying to palm one off."

"How about the cat?" said Frank. "Did you test it in any way?"

"No. It seemed authentic. Zufar offered to let me keep it for a detailed examination, but I told him we had no funds available for such a purchase at this time."

The curator paused to polish his glasses. "Then came a dreadful piece of bad luck. Zufar went to put the cat back in the carrying case—but, in his disturbed state, he let it slip from his fingers."

"Did the cat break?" Chet blurted out.

"Shattered to bits." Mr. Scath shook his head unhappily. "What followed was even worse. Zufar himself went all to pieces."

The curator related that Zufar had then begun pouring out his troubles. He told of the golden Pharaoh's head which had been lost when the *Katawa* sank, and said he had heard that the shipping line's insurance company thought he was trying to defraud them, because of some false rumor about a duplicate head.

"Did he strike you as putting on an act?" Frank asked.

"I don't believe so. He said he's had nothing but bad luck ever since the gold treasure first came into his possession. Then he asked me to recommend a good detective agency to run down the scoundrel who was defaming him. Naturally," Mr. Scath ended, "I suggested your father."

"Zufar still seemed pretty tense when he came

to our place," Joe mused. "How much is the Egyptian cat worth, Mr. Scath?"

"Hard to say. But at least five hundred dollars."

"Wow!" Chet broke in. "That's a high price for butterfingers."

"Incidentally," Mr. Scath went on, "Zufar's tale of bad luck may well be true *if* you accept superstition."

Frank said, "How so?"

"When the tomb of Rhamaton IV was opened, a curse was supposed to fall on those who had violated the royal crypt," Mr. Scath explained, "and the curse actually seemed to be fulfilled. The newspapers made much of it at the time."

"What happened?" Joe asked.

"Soon after the discovery, the leader of the excavating party died of a heart attack. And several others in the party became ill or suffered accidents."

Chet shifted uneasily.

"The Rhamaton head eventually came into the possession of a wealthy Lebanese businessman in Beirut," Mr. Scath went on. "He was later ruined financially. Then when Zufar bought the head and was bringing it to this country, the ship sank."

Frank said dryly, "Seems to bear out the curse all right, except I don't believe in ancient curses."

"Well, I'm not so sure I don't," Chet said.

After thanking the curator, the boys left the museum and drove to the beach. An hour of swimming and sunbathing, topped off by a lunch of hamburgers, soon put even Chet in a more cheerful mood.

At four-thirty that afternoon the Hardys picked up Iola, Chet, and Callie for Biff's barbecue.

The Hoopers' wide yard, which sloped down to a pleasant, woodsy creek, was already noisy with the gay chatter of boys and girls when the Hardys' group arrived.

Eager shouts greeted them. Chet was promptly given a chef's hat and apron.

"This is my style!" he said laughingly, and soon was busy stoking the portable grill.

Biff, a tall, blond, and rangy youth, ambled among his guests, handing out soft drinks. Then he cupped his big hands and bellowed for attention.

"Now hear this, you guys and gals!"

Suddenly Biff's jovial expression turned to one of dismay. Startled gasps and squeals came from the other guests.

"Joe, look out!" warned Tony Prito.

Before Joe could react, something struck him hard in the back, sending him sprawling to the ground!

CHAPTER X

A Four-legged Menace

"HEY! What gives?" Joe spluttered. He tried to get up, but felt paws trampling his back.

As he turned his head, a large wet tongue licked him across the face. His assailant was an ungainly Great Dane!

"Down, Tivoli! Here, boy!" Biff shouted as he ran to his guest's assistance. Everyone else was roaring with laughter.

Joe finally struggled to his feet. "For Pete's sake," he gasped, wiping his face, "where'd that monster come from?"

"He's no monster—he's my big surprise," said Biff, hanging on to the huge dog with both hands. "I'll have you know this magnificent creature comes from champion— *Oof!*"

Biff broke off with a grunt as the Dane pulled free from his grip and went bounding off among the young people. "Hey, come here! I said, *come,* Tivoli!"

The dog paid no attention. He pranced happily about the lawn, barging into several teenagers and spilling their soda pop. Biff pursued his pet, but the Great Dane eluded him as nimbly as a swivel-hipped quarterback.

"Watch it, Chet!" Tony Prito shouted. "He's going for the hot dogs!"

The party was in an uproar. Phil Cohen, at Biff's frantic request, ran into the house and got a chain-link training collar.

With Frank helping, Biff finally put the collar around Tivoli's neck—but not before the dog had gulped five frankfurters and a package of hamburger meat.

"Don't you ever feed the poor thing?" Tony joked.

"Feed him?" Biff said indignantly. "Listen, he's had three big meals today already!" Then he added hastily, "Tivoli's not *really* such a terribly big eater—"

A chorus of disbelieving laughs greeted his words.

"He's not!" Biff insisted. "It's just that he got half-starved when he was being shipped here, so now he's making up for lost time."

Iola giggled. "And how! I'll bet even Chet has a canary's appetite by comparison!"

"You still haven't told us how you got him, Biff," said Jim Foy, a Chinese youth.

"I won him in a mail-order contest." Biff explained that he had submitted the winning slogan for a new cereal and had received Tivoli as first prize.

"How old is the mutt?" asked Jerry Gilroy.

"Mutt my eye!" Biff retorted. "This dog comes from purebred stock. His father and mother were both international champions—and Tivoli will be, too, someday. He's just nine months old."

"Nine months?" Chet echoed. "Good night, he's as big as a colt already! How big will he be when he's full grown?"

"Big enough to make the best watchdog in Bayport," Biff said proudly. He cleared his throat. "Ahem! It just happens that Tivoli—er—arrived at a bad time, with us going on vacation. So as I was about to announce, one of you lucky people can have the privilege of keeping this future champ while I'm gone."

Another chorus of laughter arose.

"Did you say *lucky?*" teased Callie.

"Does the offer include a cage?" Phil added.

" 'Fraid you're wasting your time, Biff old pal," added another boy. "You'll have to board him at a kennel—if you can find one big enough."

Summoning up a hearty pitchman's smile, Biff went on, "Listen, gang. Think what an impression Tivoli will make when you take him out on a leash."

Tony chuckled. "He'll make an impression all right. Everybody'll run for cover."

"You'll have to admit he'd make a great guard dog," Biff persevered.

Frank turned to Joe and remarked thoughtfully, "You know, he's right. I've been worried about us leaving Aunt Gertrude alone when we go back to Whalebone Island—in case that prowler shows up again. Tivoli might be just the answer!"

Joe nodded. "You have a point there."

"Okay, Biff," Frank said in a louder voice. "You've got yourself a deal."

"You mean you'll take him?"

"For two weeks."

Biff gave a whoop of joy and the other teen-agers began crowding around the Hardys to offer joking words of warning and advice.

When the party broke up at seven-thirty, Frank and Joe drove Tivoli home in their convertible with the top up and the windows raised.

"We'd better go in first and break the news gently," Frank said as they parked in the driveway.

Joe chuckled. "We may need Tivoli to protect *us.*"

As the boys went in the front door, Aunt Gertrude came into the hallway. "Do either of you know if your father was expecting some sort of shipment?" she asked.

"A shipment?" Joe said blankly. "Of what?"

"That's just what I'm trying to find out. A crate came for him while you were gone. I didn't know what else to do with it so I had the truck driver and his helper carry it down to the basement."

"It's news to us, Aunty," said Frank. "Let's take a look."

Miss Hardy led the way down the cellar stairs. She pointed to a large wooden crate standing against the wall. It was about four feet high. Stenciled on one side was the name FENTON HARDY and the address of the Hardy home.

"What about the receipt?" Joe suggested. "Wouldn't that tell us the contents?"

"Oh dear! I forgot to ask for the carbon copy when I signed it," said Miss Hardy. "But, anyway, the handwriting on the receipt was illegible."

"Didn't the driver even know where the box came from?" Frank asked.

"He said he'd picked it up at some New York warehouse. That was all he could tell me."

Frank eyed the mysterious crate. "Maybe we should call Dad."

"Oh, I didn't neglect that," said Miss Hardy. "I tried to contact Fenton over the radio but he didn't answer."

"No wonder—his radio got smashed on Whalebone Island," Joe explained. "But we can probably call him at his hotel."

As Joe picked up the basement extension telephone, his aunt said, "Will you also tell him a man phoned about five o'clock? He didn't leave any name."

Joe placed the call to Philadelphia, but hung up with a shake of his head a few minutes later. "No luck. Dad and Sam Radley are both out of their rooms. I left a message for them to call back."

The Hardy boys looked at each other and took deep breaths.

Trying to sound casual, Frank said, "Er—we've brought a visitor, Aunt Gertrude."

"A visitor?"

"Uh—yes. He's coming to stay for a couple of weeks. We're sure you're going to like him."

Detecting something odd in Frank's tone, Miss Hardy swept her nephews with a suspicious glance. "Well, speak up. Who is he and where is he?"

"He's out in the car," Joe said. "Aunty, he's a Great Dane."

"A *Great Dane?*" Miss Hardy echoed unbelievingly. "You mean one of those—those huge dogs?"

Frank tried to be reassuring. "Actually, he's not full grown. Only nine months old."

Gertrude Hardy launched into a vigorous tirade against the problem of tending large, untrained animals. Frank finally managed to explain why they had brought Tivoli, stressing that he would serve as a watchdog while he and Joe were away.

"And just where do you expect me to keep the creature?" Miss Hardy demanded. "Certainly not in the house."

"Oh, don't worry about that, Aunty," Joe said, chuckling. "Tivoli can stay out in the yard or down in the cellar."

"Well, he'd better earn his board and keep," Aunt Gertrude commented tartly.

With that, she marched upstairs to the kitchen. Joe glanced at his brother and rolled his eyes expressively.

"Well, let's bring in our visitor," Frank said, grinning.

When the boys returned to the car, they found Tivoli comfortably lolling on the back seat, fast asleep. Joe jerked the ring on the end of his training collar. "Come on, boy. We're going to introduce you to Aunt Gertrude."

Tivoli preferred not to be disturbed. Only the combined physical persuasion of Joe and Frank succeeded in dislodging him, and even then he proved skittish. Moments later, as they were hauling him in the door, the boys heard a shriek from their aunt.

"What's wrong?" Frank called out. Tivoli now lunged for the kitchen, tugging the boys behind him.

"That prowler—he's back again!" Miss Hardy's eyes widened in fright at the sight of the Great Dane, but she went on, "I heard a noise out back and saw a man dask across the yard!"

"It's your big chance, Tivoli! Go get him!" Joe commanded.

The two boys and the dog dashed out the back door. But the prowler had vanished in the gathering dusk. Now Tivoli strained toward the house and the boys were forced to follow.

"Maybe the fellow dropped something or left a clue, and Tivoli's spotted it by scent!" Joe said hopefully.

The real reason soon became evident as the Great Dane headed for the kitchen. Once inside, he strode toward the refrigerator and began sniffing at the door.

Aunt Gertrude gave the boys a withering glance. "A fine watchdog *he'll* make!" Resolutely she advanced on Tivoli. "Outside this instant!"

The dog regarded her with its pale-yellow eyes. He made no move to obey, but a faint rumble sounded in his throat. Miss Hardy stood her ground. "Frank and Joe," she said, "take this creature out of the house! Immediately!"

Her nephews complied, and coaxed Tivoli into the back yard once more.

Joe laughed. "He's as iron-willed as Aunt Gertrude."

"Time will tell," Frank said philosophically. He

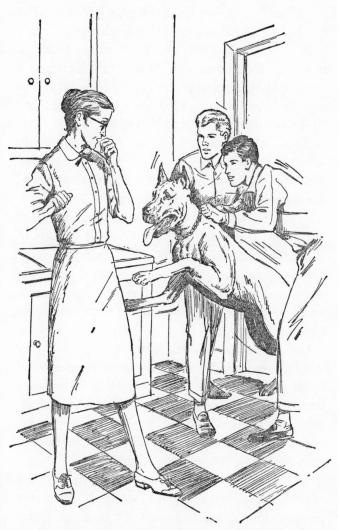

Aunt Gertrude's eyes widened in fright at sight of the
Great Dane

got a length of chain from the garage and secured one end to Tivoli's collar and the other to a tree.

Back in the kitchen, the boys had just fixed a snack for themselves and Aunt Gertrude when a mournful howl assailed their ears. They looked at each other, then glanced at Miss Hardy. Her face spoke volumes but she said nothing.

Tivoli continued to bay at the rising moon. Aunt Gertrude winced. The baying persisted without letup. After several minutes she pursed her lips and got up from the table.

"Very well. You'd better bring that so-called watchdog inside before the neighbors complain. But put him in the cellar, mind you!"

Frank and Joe did so. As they came back upstairs, Aunt Gertrude gave an indignant sniff. "Now perhaps we'll be able to get some rest. I, for one, am retiring."

She swept out of the room.

The boys finished eating, then tried several times to reach their father. No luck. They were just about to go upstairs when Tivoli came trotting into the hallway!

Joe burst out laughing. "He must be able to turn the doorknob with his jaws!"

"Oh, no, you don't!" Frank said hastily. He caught Tivoli just in time to deter the huge dog from settling himself comfortably on a newly upholstered sofa in the living room.

"You know, I'm beginning to think Aunt Gertrude is right about this pooch! He may be more hindrance than help."

"Let's give him a chance." Joe grinned. "It's only his first day here."

Frank took the Great Dane back to the cellar.

Yawning, the boys switched off the lights, turned on the burglar alarm, and went to their room.

Some time later came the sound of paws padding up the staircase. Joe raised his head from the pillow incredulously. "Good grief! Tivoli again!"

Apparently sniffing out his two protectors, the dog stalked into the boys' room. He leaped onto Joe's bed with a single bound and draped himself across the middle.

Joe groaned. "Oh great! Well, I guess you might as well stay here so we can get some sleep. But at least give me a little room, you big lummox."

Frank shook with stifled laughter.

It was past midnight when the boys were suddenly awakened by the loud barking noise of Tivoli from downstairs. They heard the dog snarl —then the sounds of a violent struggle.

"Come on!" Frank exclaimed, jumping out of bed. "Let's find out what's going on!"

CHAPTER XI

A Clever Dodge

THE boys sped downstairs in their pajamas to investigate the commotion. As Frank switched on the light, Joe let out a gasp. "Look! Tivoli!"

The Great Dane lay sprawled across the threshold of the guest room! The brothers ran to the dog.

Frank and Joe experienced pangs of fear upon seeing that Tivoli was motionless. But closer examination showed the Dane was breathing. Then Joe's eyes fell on Captain Early's carved cane lying on the floor nearby. "Someone beaned him with that stick!"

"And got away!" Frank said, pointing to the open window of the guest room. Both boys dashed toward it and Frank thrust out his head.

The stillness was unbroken except for the thrum of crickets. There was no sign of the intruder.

As the boys turned back to the unconscious dog, Aunt Gertrude arrived on the scene, wearing a bathrobe and hair net. "Mercy! What on earth has happened?"

Frank said, "Someone broke in. Tivoli went for him, but got conked."

Miss Hardy drew in her breath sharply. "The nasty brute!"

"Tivoli?"

"No, the dreadful person who struck him!"

"Poor old fellow!" Joe squatted down beside the Great Dane. "Wonder what you do for an unconscious dog. Give him smelling salts?"

"Don't be ridiculous," Aunt Gertrude said tartly. "I'll attend to this brave creature."

Joe rose to his feet and exchanged amused glances with his brother. Aunt Gertrude's change of attitude toward Tivoli was a pleasant surprise.

"What I'd like to know," Frank said thoughtfully, "is how the prowler got inside without touching off the burglar alarm."

"It's still on!" Joe reported, after glancing at the wall switch in the hallway. "That must mean the alarm system is dead!"

The boys rushed to the cellar to inspect the master control panel. When Frank opened the switch box, the answer was immediately evident. A wire had been disconnected!

"Who did that?" Joe exclaimed.

"It sure didn't come loose by itself." Frank frowned. "Remember that fellow Aunt Gertrude saw running across the back yard? He may have been coming from the cellar, after having yanked this wire loose so he'd have a clear field tonight."

"Hmm. Could be, if one of the cellar windows isn't fastened."

The boys examined each of the four windows. The catch on one in the rear was unhooked!

"This is the way somebody got out," Frank said. "But how did he get in? I checked all these windows when you were telephoning Philadelphia— and they were locked."

Joe looked baffled and leaned against the crate. "Maybe he just oozed through the walls."

Frank had to admit he couldn't figure out an answer, but added, "There is a way, and we're going to find out."

The young sleuths went back upstairs. In the kitchen they halted in astonishment. Tivoli was devouring a pan of stew. Aunt Gertrude occasionally would bathe the bruise on his head with a damp cloth. The dog stopped eating long enough to give the boys a brief look of content.

"Poor thing," Aunt Gertrude murmured. "Such a stouthearted protector deserves a good meal."

Tivoli happily continued gulping the stew.

As the boys went back to the guest room to search for clues, Joe said with a chuckle, "Boy, what a change! Aunt Gertrude can't do enough for him."

Frank smiled. "I guess she's convinced his heart's in the right place."

Neither the room nor the carved cane yielded any fingerprints, nor had the intruder left any trace of his identity. Presently the boys and Aunt Gertrude returned to their rooms. Frank and Joe noticed with amusement that their aunt had said nothing further about putting the Great Dane back in the cellar.

Early the next morning while Miss Hardy was preparing breakfast the telephone rang. Fenton Hardy was calling from Philadelphia. "Sam and I didn't get back to the hotel until one this morning," he explained, "so I decided to wait till later to phone you fellows back. What's up?"

Joe hastily reported the midnight break-in and the delivery, earlier, of the mysterious crate.

Mr. Hardy was perplexed. "I've no idea what's in it," he said. "You and Frank had better open it right away. Then call me back."

Eagerly the boys went down to the basement, where they got a claw hammer and pry bar to rip open the crate. To their amazement, one side of the box suddenly dropped like a trap door! Empty!

The Hardys stared at each other, speechless; then at the crate. "Are you thinking what I am?" Joe asked.

"There must have been a man hiding in here!" Frank exclaimed, indicating the hinged side of the crate, which had an inner hook. "After he got out, he wedged the side in place."

"Then he was all set to rob the house!"

"Sure," agreed Frank. "But when he heard you telling Aunt Gertrude the dog could stay down here, he decided to scram before Tivoli could detect him. So he ducked out the cellar window."

"You're right!" Joe said, snapping his fingers. "But first he disconnected the burglar alarm so he could get back in later."

With a puzzled look, Joe added, "This crate gag seems like an awfully elaborate dodge for a house-breaker."

"It was an ingenious way to sneak past our alarm system," Frank pointed out. "He learned about that when he tried to break in while we were away on Whalebone Island."

Frank promptly telephoned his father to report the boys' discovery.

"You're sure nothing was taken last night?" Mr. Hardy asked.

"Not as far as we could find out, Dad," Frank replied. "I think Tivoli jumped the fellow too fast. Then he heard us coming and had to scram."

"Hmm. So we're still in the dark about what he was after."

The detective was keenly interested when Frank went on to describe Mehmet Zufar's visit. "I'd certainly like to know more about this alleged defamation of character he complains of," Mr. Hardy mused. "It might open up some new angles on the Pharaoh's head mystery."

"Then why not take the case for Zufar?" Frank proposed. "He's eager to engage a top-flight detective."

"That wouldn't be ethical, son. I could hardly go to work for Zufar when he's already under suspicion in the matter I'm investigating for Transmarine Underwriters. From what you say, he evidently doesn't know about my assignment."

Joe, who was listening with one ear close to the phone, broke in. "But, Dad, why should there be any conflict? If Zufar is on the level, he wants the Pharaoh's head mystery cleared up as much as you do."

Mr. Hardy was silent for a moment. Then he said, "Tell you what. Suppose you fellows go to New York and talk to Zufar again. Tell him I'm not at liberty to take his case just now, but I'll try to help as soon as possible if he'll give you fellows all the facts."

"Swell idea!" Frank agreed. "Maybe we can pick up some good leads!"

"Incidentally," Mr. Hardy added, "I think Sam should be free this afternoon. He'll fly to Bayport and the three of you can go to Whalebone Island as we planned."

"Great!"

Both Frank and Joe were eager for the trip to New York. After a hasty breakfast they drove to the railroad station and caught an early train. By ten minutes after eleven they were stepping out of a taxi at Zufar's address in Lower Manhattan.

The address proved to be a grimy loft building. On the card Zufar had given them he had also written the name *"Fritz Bogdan, Curio Dealer."* The same name was lettered on the windows of a ground-floor shop.

Frank and Joe entered the shop and found themselves in a long, dimly lighted room filled with Oriental carpets, statuary, paintings, and curios.

A tall, hawk-faced man with iron-gray hair eyed them curiously.

"May I help you?"

"Are you Mr. Bogdan?" Frank asked. When the man nodded, he went on, "We're looking for Mr. Mehmet Zufar."

"Oh, yes. I'm his American agent. He occupies office space here on his visits to this country."

Bogdan led the boys past a huge green Buddha figure to an inner corridor and pointed to an office doorway bearing Zufar's name. Frank thanked Bogdan and rapped on the door.

"Come in!"

Zufar looked up startled from his desk as the Hardys entered. He listened with obvious impatience as Frank repeated what Mr. Hardy had said. Then he pounded a fist on the desk.

"Now listen! Something has come up that changes everything. Your father must help me!"

CHAPTER XII

Key 273

THE mustached art dealer's reaction took the Hardys by surprise.

"Do you have some kind of clue?" Frank asked.

Zufar's eyes narrowed. "A good deduction." His fingers nervously plucked an envelope from his desk. "This letter came in the morning mail," he said, handing it over. "See for yourself."

Frank took the envelope, which bore a typewritten address and was postmarked New York, N. Y. Inside was a note and a small key stamped with the number 273.

The note, which also was typed, read:

> *We have the gold head of Rhamaton IV.*
> *We will sell it back to you for $100,000.*
> *Be ready with your answer. SHOW THIS*
> *NOTE TO NO ONE IF YOU VALUE*
> *YOUR LIFE!*

The Hardys exchanged baffled glances.

"If the gang who sent this have the Pharaoh's head, Mr. Zufar," said Joe, "why should they offer to sell it back to *you?*"

The dealer mopped his brow with a lavender silk handkerchief. "Who knows? Maybe the thieves have been unable to find a private buyer willing to pay such a price for a stolen art object. Do not forget—the deal would entail great risk on both sides, and the buyer would never be able to display his acquisition."

"Maybe," Frank suggested, "the thieves think you're aiming to collect from the insurance company, then sell the head secretly for much *more* than a hundred thousand."

Zufar shot him a sharp glance. "It is possible," he admitted grudgingly.

"Do you think it's likely that the persons who sent the note really have the authentic head?" Joe inquired.

The dealer threw up his hands in despair. "Alas, I fear so. The head may have been salvaged from the *Katawa*'s strong room, or stolen or switched by some trickery before the ship left port."

"Would there have been time for anyone to do either?" Frank asked.

"Of course. I purposely arranged to have the head brought aboard several hours before any passengers embarked, in order not to attract attention. That was in Beirut. Again there was a chance for trickery when we stopped at Le Havre. If the purser was dishonest—who knows?"

Zufar shrugged unhappily. The purser, he added, had been lost in the sinking.

Frank replaced the note in its envelope, then said, "Personally, I think you should take this note to the police, Mr. Zufar."

The art dealer's eyes bulged fearfully. "You think I am a fool?" he said shrilly. "If I did, my life would be in danger!"

"But you've showed the note to us," Frank pointed out.

"That is different. Your father is not the police. If these—these thieves contact me, I can say simply that I have hired him to act as my go-between."

Dabbing his face with the handkerchief, Zufar went on, "Furthermore, once this became an official matter for the police, the news might leak out. I cannot afford to endanger my reputation any further!"

The telephone on Zufar's desk rang. "Excuse me."

He scooped it up. "Hello? . . . Yes, this is Mehmet Zufar speaking."

Suddenly the dealer's face grew pale. He beckoned frantically to the Hardys and held the telephone away from his ear so they could listen in.

"You heard me! Speak up!" a harsh voice was saying on the other end of the line. "I asked if you're ready to make a deal."

Zufar looked pleadingly at the boys.

Frank and Joe hesitated. Then, with a glance of mutual understanding, reached a quick decision. Frank nodded emphatically.

Zufar gave a sigh of relief. "Very well," he said into the receiver. "What do you wish me to do?"

"Listen carefully. Have the money ready in small bills. Take that key to the Philadelphia Airport. Use it to open a public-storage locker there and stand by."

There was a sudden click as the caller hung up. Zufar, too, put down the phone and turned his eyes to the Hardys. "You keep the note and the key, and you will inform your father immediately?"

"We'll get in touch with him," Frank promised, pocketing the envelope. "Good-by."

Frank and Joe left the office. In the corridor they almost bumped into Fritz Bogdan. The proprietor gave them a thin smile and walked on quickly down the hall to a rear storage room.

As the boys went through the display area, their gaze swept over the exotic assortment of merchandise. A tigerskin rug hung on one wall between dusty carpets and tapestries. Near the green Buddha, the painted face of an Egyptian mummy case stared back at them sightlessly. Both boys felt there was something sinister about the dingy place.

An employee was moving a large, murky-colored landscape painting in a gold frame. The Hardys recognized him as Zufar's granite-faced chauffeur.

When they reached the street, Joe muttered, "Do you suppose that fellow Bogdan was eavesdropping?"

"Don't know. I was wondering the same thing," Frank replied. "You know, I have a feeling I've seen him somewhere before."

"Me too. I thought his face seemed sort of familiar."

Neither of the Hardys could explain the impression.

"Well," Frank said, "we'd better get in touch with Dad and then get a bite to eat. I could sure use a couple of hamburgers."

Sighting a drugstore on the next corner, the boys went inside where Frank phoned their father. Mr. Hardy readily approved of his sons' action.

"Don't worry, you and Joe used good judgment," he said. "The Philadelphia Airport angle strikes me as a good omen, too."

"How so, Dad?"

"There are only a few private collectors in the eastern United States who might be avid enough and rich enough to buy something like the gold Pharaoh's head, even if it was stolen," the detective explained. "The two most likely purchasers live within fifty miles of Philadelphia. That's why

Sam and I have been concentrating on this area."

"Sure hope this lead pays off," Frank said. "What's our next move, Dad?"

Fenton Hardy instructed the boys to take the letter with the key to La Guardia Airport and leave it with a friend who worked for one of the airlines. Sam Radley, he went on, would fly there, pick up the envelope, and bring it back to Philadelphia.

Frank asked, "Does that mean Sam won't be coming to Bayport this afternoon?"

"I may need his help on this new development with Zufar," Mr. Hardy said. "Anyhow, I've made a slight change of plans for you fellows." Excited, Frank signaled Joe close to the receiver.

"The Crux Diving Company's salvage ship is leaving New York today to begin operations on the *Katawa*. Captain Rankin has agreed to take you and Joe along and drop you on Whalebone Island."

The vessel would be close at hand in case of emergency, the detective added. They could pursue the Jolly Roger's mystery and keep in touch with the salvage operations.

"That's great, Dad!" said Frank. "But wouldn't it be better if we had the *Sleuth* along with its radio?"

After a hasty discussion, they decided that Joe

would board the Crux ship alone. Frank would return to Bayport, get Chet and the *Sleuth,* and then proceed to Whalebone Island.

After a quick lunch at a coffee shop, the Hardys split up. Frank headed for La Guardia Airport, while Joe went straight to the pier where the Crux ship, *Petrel,* lay berthed.

The dock was bustling with activity as supplies were loaded aboard. Joe hurried toward the gangplank to announce himself to the deck officer.

A heavy oil drum, slung from a cargo hook, was just being hoisted from the pier. Joe passed underneath as the boom swung inward toward the ship's hold.

"Hey! Watch it!"

Joe whirled at the sudden cry of alarm. In that instant the oil drum plunged straight toward his head!

CHAPTER XIII

A Lost Anchor

As JOE whirled around, somebody rammed him hard. He reeled backward under the impact, and together with his tackler sprawled on the dock as the oil drum crashed inches from them.

"Sufferin' snakes!" Stunned, Joe sat up limply. His thumping pulse almost blurred out the ensuing shouts and confusion.

The man who had rescued him—a husky, middle-aged six-footer in dungarees—called over reassuringly, "Take it easy, lad. No harm done." He got up nimbly and helped Joe to his feet.

"Thanks . . . thanks a lot," Joe gasped. "You saved my life."

The man's freckled face broke into a grin. "Maybe you saved mine. I was rushing across the dock and had to slow down when you got in my way. If you hadn't, I'd have been right under that drum myself!"

Meantime, stevedores had captured the dented rolling drum and were wrestling it back into position while a crewman examined the hoisting sling.

The captain shouted wrathfully from the ship, "How'd it happen, bos'n?"

"Chine hook seems to have fractured, sir! Never seen one give like that before!" Red-faced, the bos'n aimed a torrent of salty comments at the loading crew for not having spotted the cracked hook when they rigged the sling.

"You there, young fellow!" the captain called down to Joe. "You one of Fenton Hardy's boys, by any chance?"

"Yes, sir! I'm Joe Hardy—my brother won't be making the trip." Accompanied by his rescuer, Joe mounted the gangplank and shook hands with the tall, lean officer.

"Welcome aboard! I'm Captain Rankin. Sorry about the accident."

"Guess I should've kept a sharper eye out."

"Cargo handling can be as dangerous as salvage work sometimes," the skipper acknowledged. "This bucko who saved you, by the way, is our master diver, Roland Perry. He's used to danger. That's how his hair got so thin."

Perry chuckled and touched the sun-bleached reddish fuzz on his freckled pate. "Don't believe him, Joe. It's the chow they serve and the hard time he gives us salvage boys that made my hair fall out."

Joe laughed, and soon he and Perry were engaged in friendly conversation. The diver had first learned his trade at the Navy's Deep-Sea Diving School in Washington, D. C.

Late that afternoon, the ship, secured for sea after loading, churned away from its pier. Captain Rankin allowed Joe to come up on the bridge and watch as they sailed out through the busy waters of the Port of New York.

The next day Perry gave Joe a guided tour of the *Petrel*. The steel salvage vessel, he explained, was of a type specially designed by the Navy for offshore salvage work and carried equipment for handling any imaginable marine emergency.

Its electronic gear included radio, radar, loran, radiotelephone, fathometer, and radio direction finder. On its main deck was a salvage workshop with a forge, welding machine, lathe, pipe-threading machine, and various other equipment. In the engine room was a complete machine shop.

"Our towing engine has a forty-thousand-pound-line pull capacity—we can make lifts over the bow sheaves up to a hundred and fifty tons," Perry went on proudly. "We can pump more than a million gallons of water an hour—furnish electric power to a disabled vessel—and there are two miles of steel cable in our wire stowage room."

"Wow! Some setup!" said Joe, much impressed.

The diver chuckled. "We're really a floating construction warehouse. We carry everything from nuts and bolts to a concrete mixer—not to mention timbers for making patches to seal off holes in ships' hulls."

Joe was fascinated when Perry showed him the diving locker, forward on the main deck. It held several sets of diving suits, scuba gear, submarine telephone equipment, underwater burning torches, and a full stock of spare parts.

"Does Captain Rankin boss the diving operations?" Joe asked.

"No. When we reach the salvage scene, Matt Shane, our salvage master, takes over. Under him is a salvage foreman, myself, my tender, a pump engineer, a carpenter, and nine wreckers—the specialized salvage workers, that is."

It was nightfall when the *Petrel* reached curving Whalebone Island and dropped anchor in the cove. Another ship—which Joe recognized immediately as the *Simon Salvor*—was lying to the southward. But the *Salvor* was now in a different position from where it had been when the Hardys first visited the island.

"What do you suppose they're doing?" Joe asked, scanning the *Salvor* through field glasses.

"Good question, son." Matt Shane, the grizzled salvage master, chewed thoughtfully on his pipe.

"There's no wreck in that area, or we'd know about it. Salvage men keep pretty close tabs on such matters."

Roland Perry growled, "Something phony about them being here, if you ask me. Could be they came to throw a monkey wrench into *our* operations. I wouldn't put anything past Bock!"

"Take it easy, Rollie," said Shane.

Joe was startled by the mention of the Simon Salvage Company diver. "Do you know Gus Bock, Rollie?" he asked.

"Do I *know* him?" Perry snorted. "We were shipmates once on a tin can, the *Svenson*. Later on, we went through Navy diving school together. When we finally got out of service, we worked for the same salvage outfit. I actually thought we were buddies—till the time I caught him trying to split my air hose!"

The incident had occurred when both men were on the bottom, searching for a sealed cashbox aboard a sunken hulk.

"You could've been mistaken, Rollie," Shane cautioned. "Just because he had his knife in his hand—"

"I tell you I saw him going for my air line! He's a slimy shark, that Bock!"

Joe put in, "If you were on the *Svenson* with him, you must have served under Captain Phil Early."

The diver nodded. "For a while, right at the

end of the war. The skipper was transferred to another command a few months after I joined the ship. Good old Pearly Early!"

"How'd he get that nickname?" Joe asked with a grin. "From his first initial and last name?"

"That was part of it." Perry chuckled. "Ever been in Greece?"

"No. Why?"

"Over there, you'll see Greek men fussing with what they call 'worry beads.' They carry these beads and finger them all the time. Captain Early did the same thing—only he used pearls."

"Real ones?" Joe asked in surprise.

"Sure, he collected them. Had some beauties he'd picked up in the South Pacific. In fact, when he was transferred, the crew gave him a cane—"

"A cane?" Joe cut in. "How come?"

"To carry the pearls in. The handle unscrewed, you see, and there was a hollow space inside. It was specially made, and handsomely carved by our old quartermaster."

Joe's brain was in a whirl, thinking of the burglary attempts.

"What's the matter, lad?" Matt Shane asked, noticing his odd reaction.

"Funny coincidence. Captain Early's a family friend of ours, and I've seen that cane. In fact, he left it at our house."

Since there was no sign of a campfire on the island or any light in the Whalebone tower, it was apparent Frank and Chet had not yet arrived, so Joe did not ask to be put ashore.

At daybreak the next morning, when he awoke in his bunk, Joe heard the muted throb of the ship's engines and sounds of frenzied activity on deck. He hurried topside to see what was going on.

In the water nearby was one of the ship's lifeboats. While two seamen rowed it slowly, Roland Perry peered over the gunwale into a glass-bottomed box, which enabled him to see the shallow ocean floor.

"What's Rollie doing?" Joe asked Shane.

"Looking for our bower anchor. We lost it during the night."

"Good grief!" Joe exclaimed. "How'd that happen?"

Shane grinned wryly. "That's what the old man would like to know."

Joe could see Captain Rankin standing on the wing of the bridge, tight-jawed with fury over the mishap.

After a while Perry located the anchor. Donning scuba gear, he went down to reconnect the anchor to its chain. By the time the job was completed, almost half the morning had been spent.

"Someone took apart the detachable link on the swivel shot of the chain!" Rollie explained to Joe after returning topside.

"But who?"

"Who do *you* think?" the diver retorted with an angry scowl seaward at the *Simon Salvor*. "It could only have been done by a frogman. Captain Rankin has already been on the radio to the *Salvor*, but all he got was a horselaugh."

Joe mulled over the mystery. Were Gus Bock and his mates responsible for the loss of the anchor —or had someone else been the saboteur and swum out from the island under cover of darkness? If the latter was the case, Joe reflected, Red Rogers' "ghost" might have returned to Whalebone!

Much as he would have liked to watch the search for the *Katawa* get under way, Joe asked to be put ashore. He waved good-by from the cove as the *Petrel* sailed out around the island toward the scene of the sinking. Then he began to scout cautiously for possible traces of another occupant on Whalebone.

Shortly before noon Joe heard the put-put of a motorboat engine. He dashed to the cove in time to see Frank and Chet just beaching the *Sleuth*.

"Hi, you guys!" Joe shouted to them.

"Hi, Joe!"

"What cooks, Robinson Crusoe?" Chet asked.

"Not lunch, if that's what you were hoping," Joe replied with a grin. "How come it took you so long to get here?"

Frank explained that Chet had been unable to leave until late Saturday afternoon. "I figured we could stop off overnight at Captain Early's, but he wasn't home so we had to sleep on the beach."

"Did you bring the captain's cane?" Joe asked, his voice suddenly tense.

"Sure, I wanted to give it back to him, but—say, what's so special about that cane?"

As Frank and Chet stared in surprise, Joe told what he had learned about the captain's collection of pearls and the hollow receptacle in the cane. "That's what the burglar must have been after all the time!"

Frank hastily fished the cane out of the *Sleuth*. Sure enough, a metal ring showed where the cane came apart in two pieces!

Joe and Chet watched eagerly as he unscrewed the handle, then peered into the hollow.

"Well—?"

Frank turned the cane barrel upside down and shook it. "Empty. The pearls are gone!"

CHAPTER XIV

A Cave Clue

A DISMAYED silence followed Frank's discovery that the captain's cane was empty.

Then Chet spoke up. "Are you sure the pearls were in there?"

"All I know," Joe said, "is what Roland Perry told me—that the captain collected pearls and his crew had that cane specially made for him to keep them in. Besides, don't you remember last Tuesday after his house was broken into, he said there was nothing in it of value except the silver?"

"If you're right," Frank said thoughtfully, "whoever broke into our place Thursday night must have had time to remove the pearls before Tivoli attacked him!"

"Sure," Joe reasoned, "and that would explain the mystery of what our intruder was after."

Gloomily Frank screwed the cane together again. "Well, there's nothing we can do about it now. We'll just have to tell Captain Early as soon as we get in touch with him."

Frank put the cane back in the boat and began unloading sleeping bags, supplies, and scuba gear. "First of all, let's lug this stuff over to the light-house. We can use that as our base."

"Fine," Joe agreed. "And we'd better hide the *Sleuth* again, too—just in case."

The boys could not carry the entire load in a single trip, so after leaving Chet at the tower to prepare lunch, the Hardys returned to the cove for the remainder of their gear. Then the three ate with hearty appetites all the frankfurters and beans which Chet dished out, sizzling, on tin plates.

Afterward, Frank proposed another systematic search of the island. "If that fake ghost stayed here," he pointed out, "we ought to be able to find *some* evidence."

"Good idea," Joe said.

Starting out from the headland, the boys began slowly working their way around the shore of the entire crescent-shaped island.

They found no trace of other boat landings, so they started combing the inland areas.

"Hey! Fresh water!" Joe announced as they came to a tiny spring trickling out of a hillside. Hot and perspiring from the trek, he cupped his hands and bent down to scoop up a drink.

Chet couldn't resist some fun. "How about a

good face-wash, too?" Gleefully he gave Joe a prod
with the toe of his sneaker.

With a cry of surprise, Joe tried to catch his
balance. No luck. He lurched forward, lost his

footing, and plunged headfirst out of sight into a
mass of brush on the other side of the spring.

"Hey! Where'd he go?" Chet exclaimed. He and
Frank ran to the spot where Joe had vanished. Up

popped a blond head through the thick vegetation.

"Look here!" Joe shouted, beckoning excitedly. "I landed in a cave. Come on. Let's look this over."

All three crowded into the well-concealed cavern mouth and Frank took out a flashlight. Its beam revealed a cavity about twenty feet in length.

"Oh—oh!" Joe gasped. "Someone has been here, all right!" He pointed to the charred remnants of a cooking fire. Nearby was a scatter of small bird bones and rusty food cans.

"Boy, this place gives me the willies!" Chet muttered.

As Frank played his light upward from the floor, the boys saw a series of whitish marks on the wall of the cave—evidently scratched there with a piece of limestone.

"Tally marks!" said Frank. The scratches were in groups of six, each group crossed with a seventh line. "Whoever stayed here must have kept count of the days and weeks that way."

"Wow!" Chet said. "He must have lived here quite a while!"

Frank nodded. "Yes, but from the looks of things, it must have been a long time ago, so he couldn't have been the 'ghost' who tried to blow us up."

"You're right," Joe said. "Still, this might explain the spook that drove the lighthouse keeper Tang out of his mind."

"Could be," Frank agreed. "Maybe some fugitive from the law hid out here."

"Or some hermit," Joe added, "who only wanted to get away from it all."

Chet shuddered. "Imagine being alone at night in that lighthouse with some creep prowling around."

"*You* think about it," Joe quipped. "It'll give you food for thought when we turn in tonight, in place of your usual bedtime snack."

"Cut it out," Frank advised, grinning, "or all three of us may start seeing things."

By the time the adventurers pushed their way back through the entrance of the gloomy hideout, it was late in the afternoon, and gathering clouds in the southwest hid the sun. The boys marked the location of the cave with a stake, which Chet drove into the sand. Then they decided to cruise out to the *Petrel* before supper to check on the progress of the salvage operations.

Hauling the *Sleuth* out of its hiding place, they launched it into the surf and Frank started the motor. The sleek craft put-putted out of the cove, then around the island and northward to the ship.

"That sky's getting darker," Joe commented.

"Wind's whipping up, too," said Frank. "We'd better not stay out too long. We might have a rough time getting back."

Soon the *Petrel* came sharply into view and the companions saw that a boom for a diving stage had been rigged out. Frank brought their motorboat alongside and Joe made fast a line.

"Ahoy there! Coming aboard!" Chet called up. When a head popped over the side, they climbed a series of steel rungs onto the deck.

Captain Rankin greeted them cordially and shook hands with Frank and Chet as Joe made the introductions.

"Have you located the *Katawa* yet, sir?" Joe asked.

"Not yet. Rollie's down on the bottom right now. Follow me."

He led the boys around to the portside where the diving crew was standing by, under the command of Matt Shane. Here the young sleuths met Perry's tender, a husky Negro named Sid Carter, who was manning the undersea telephone. The return phone lead was plugged into a loud-speaker.

Carter smiled at the boys and jabbed a finger toward the bottom. "Rollie's been down long enough to have found Davy Jones himself."

"It's slow going," Matt commented, his eyes glued to the bubbles erupting on the sloping green waves.

Suddenly Perry's voice came through: "Think I see her! . . . Wait—yes! It's the *Katawa,* all right!"

"Nice going!" said Joe.

Matt hastily donned a headset. "How is she positioned, Rollie?"

There was a moment's hesitation. "Way over on her portside—almost bottom up. Looks like quite a mess. The *Carona* really sliced her!"

Silence again as the diver made his way closer to the wreck. Suddenly there was a startled exclamation, and Perry's voice crackled over the speaker:

"Matt! Someone got here before us."

"What do you mean?"

"There's a hole cut in her side!"

CHAPTER XV

Trouble Ashore

So the *Katawa* had been raided by an unauthorized diver! Frank's and Joe's eyes widened. Did this explain how the golden Pharaoh's head had come into the possession of the thieves who sent the ransom note to Zufar?

"Where was the hole cut, Rollie?" the salvage master called down.

"Can't see too clearly, Matt, till I get closer— but it looks from here like the engine room."

The Hardys and Chet clung tightly to the rail as a gust of wind swept the ship. The sea was getting rougher by the moment. They saw the radioman emerge from his shack and hurry across the deck to speak to Captain Rankin. The captain listened and glanced at the threatening sky, then came over and spoke to Matt Shane.

"That hurricane's veering our way, Matt. We'll just get the fringes, I think, but it may be pretty hard to hold our station. Can you secure from diving for now?"

"Sure, Cap'n. We've found the wreck—that's the main thing. Rollie can start fresh in the morning and get the lay o' things inside."

Orders were called down for the diver to come aboard the stage, or platform. After the *Petrel* dropped a marker buoy, the slow process of raising Perry to the surface began.

Being experienced scuba divers, the Hardys knew that this was done gradually to prevent a diver from suffering an attack of the bends, caused by nitrogen bubbles forming in the blood when a diver is decompressed too quickly.

By the time Perry stepped aboard from the diving stage, the sky was almost as dark as night and the ship rolled and pitched violently.

The *Sleuth*, meanwhile, had been hoisted aboard. At Captain Rankin's invitation, the boys had decided to return to the island on the salvage ship.

Perry sat on the diver's stool while his tender unsuited him. Joe introduced Frank and Chet to Perry as soon as his helmet was removed.

"From the looks of this weather, I should have stayed at the bottom," Perry remarked.

Bucking heavy seas, the *Petrel* plowed back to Whalebone Island. Soon after it had dropped anchor in the cove, the *Simon Salvor* also put in for shelter. Gale-force winds were now bending the trees on shore, and within minutes solid sheets of rain came lashing down on the two ships.

Frank and Joe enjoyed a hearty dinner in the crew's mess. But, for once, Chet seemed to lack appetite. He said nothing, but his pals guessed the heaving motions of the ship were responsible.

"Say, I wonder if Captain Early might be home by now," Joe mused.

"Maybe," Frank said. "Why?"

"We might be able to contact him by ship-to-shore telephone. I'd like to find out for sure about those pearls."

"So would I—if we can get along the deck without being blown overboard."

"Wind's died down quite a bit," Sid Carter spoke up. "Go ahead—you can make it to the radio shack without any trouble."

Chet, welcoming the chance for fresh air, accompanied the Hardys as they scooted forward, hugging the deckhousing for shelter. The rain, too, had abated, and the boys reached the radio compartment without much difficulty.

The radioman, Harry Egner, readily agreed to put through their call. In a few moments Captain Early was on the line.

Frank related their theory that the pearls might have been the object of the burglary attempts and told how they had found the cane to be empty.

"Don't worry. I haven't carried any pearls in the

cane since I retired from the Service," Captain Early replied. "You fellows deserve credit for a smart guess, though."

The captain explained that the pearls which he had collected had been made into a necklace for his late wife, and now were owned by one of her relatives.

Frank, somewhat letdown, observed, "Even so, the burglar must have thought the cane still held a fortune in pearls, just as we did."

"Hmm. I suppose that's possible," Captain Early agreed, "if he'd heard about me from some acquaintance in the Navy."

"One thing has us stymied," Frank went on. "How did he know the cane was still at our house? If he trailed you there Monday night and saw you leave the next day, I should think he would've been fooled by seeing you carry Dad's walking stick."

"Hold on! Maybe he *was!*" Captain Early said excitedly. "You remember my telling you about that motorist who picked me up?"

"Yes."

"The fellow seemed interested in my cane— even asked to take a look at it after I got into his car. It was then I first noticed I'd taken the wrong one, and I mentioned the mix-up."

"Wow! That could mean he drained the gas tank Monday night!" Frank exclaimed. "He may have counted on picking you up when you ran out of gas, swiping your cane, and pushing you out of the car!"

Joe, who was listening in on the conversation, broke in, "So he knew where to look for the cane— at our house."

"Well, boys, your theory seems to explain all the angles of the case," Captain Early said. "At any rate, the burglar hasn't come back. And I hope he doesn't."

Frank ended the call after getting a description of the motorist and his car.

The rain ceased and the skies began to clear soon after the boys emerged from the radio shack. Roland Perry met them out on deck.

"Looks as though we're in luck," he remarked. "Captain says the hurricane's moving out to sea again."

"Hmm! That air sure smells good," said Chet, who was rapidly regaining his usual healthy appetite. "Think I'll go see if the cook has any leftovers."

"Watch it. He may put you to work washing dishes," Joe joked.

"Who cares? It'll be worth it!" Chet said breezily, and trotted off toward the galley.

Stars were now twinkling brightly and the cove lay silvered with moonlight. Voices carried across the water from the *Salvor* anchored nearby.

Perry eyed the other boat suspiciously. "I'd sure

give a lot to know what those bilge rats are after."

The Hardys, recalling Bock's threat to their father, expressed the same interest. Frank then told the diver about the cave on the island. "It looks as if somebody lived in it."

"And it may be the answer to a ghost mystery," Joe stated. "You want to have a look at it?"

Perry, intrigued, quickly agreed to accompany the Hardys ashore. The *Sleuth* was lowered over the side and a few spurts of her motor brought them quickly to the beach.

When they reached the cave, Frank led the way inside. He shone his flashlight beam over the campsite traces on the floor, then upward to the tally marks scratched on the wall.

"Poor guy. Must have had a pretty rugged diet," said Perry, toeing the scattered bird bones. "I'd say he was probably a shipwrecked sailor or a stranded fisherman."

"In that case, why live in a cave when there's a perfectly good lighthouse handy?" Joe countered.

"Hmm, you have a point there." The diver rubbed his jaw thoughtfully. "What's this ghost mystery you mentioned?"

"A lighthouse keeper here years ago claimed he saw—" Suddenly Joe broke off and pointed to the mouth of the cave.

A glow of light was visible outside!

Perry strode through the cave entrance, Joe and Frank pressing close behind. A dazzling glare struck their eyes. The boys countered with their own flashlights, revealing two figures in the darkness. One was a lanky, baldheaded man with tufted, sandy eyebrows.

The other was Gus Bock!

"Well, well! I might've known," Perry said coldly. "Sneaky as ever—eh, Bock?"

The burly diver's face took on an ugly scowl. He shot a glance at Frank and Joe and grunted. The boys saw his hamlike fists clenched.

"Stow it, Perry!"

"Maybe you'd like to tell us what you're doing here," Perry retorted. "Besides eavesdropping, that is."

Bock advanced, his jaw jutting furiously. "Maybe *you'd* like a mouthful of knuckles!"

"*Nein*, Bock! *Lass das!*" With a guttural growl, the baldheaded man tried to hold back his companion. "We do not want trouble!"

"He's asking for it!" Bock shook off the man's restraining hand.

"Looks as if we don't have to ask," Perry said evenly. "Someone slipped our anchor for us last night."

Bock let out a hoot of raucous laughter, but it broke off abruptly, as Perry added, "At least that's a change from cutting air hoses."

With a snarl, Bock hurled a punch at his former

shipmate. Perry ducked fast enough so the blow only grazed his jaw. Then his own fist smashed out at Bock and the burly diver went sprawling on the ground.

Bock's face was contorted with rage as he picked himself up. "Okay, Perry! This time you really get the works!"

"Hold it!"

Everyone turned at the barked-out order. Captain Rankin had materialized out of the darkness, accompanied by his brawny bos'n.

"That'll be enough!" Rankin's tone of command had the desired effect. Bock froze sullenly. "On your way, you two."

"We'll go—for now," Bock snarled. "But I ain't finished with you, Perry." He glared at Frank and Joe. "And you better watch it, too."

He turned and slunk off with his companion.

Perry watched until they were out of earshot, then said to Captain Rankin, "What's the idea, skipper? You on shore patrol?"

"You might call it that, Rollie. I saw Bock and his friend go ashore after you three did and figured there might be trouble. Seems I was right."

Perry retorted dryly, "Bock and I are in for a showdown sooner or later."

Frank told the men of the hostile diver's visit to their home. Rankin looked concerned and suggested, "Maybe you boys had better bunk on board tonight—just to be on the safe side."

The Hardys accepted, eager to learn what Perry would find on his next descent to the *Katawa*.

The next morning they tried to persuade the diver and Matt Shane to let them accompany Perry down and help search the hulk.

Shane shook his head. "Not a chance, lads. The engine room's one of the most dangerous places for a diver to go on a wreck. It's a regular tangle of pipes and machinery, and the spilled oil makes it twice as hazardous."

"At least let us watch," Frank pleaded. "We've had plenty of experience scuba diving, and we'll promise not to go aboard."

Shane and Perry finally gave consent. The Hardys made a quick trip ashore with Chet to retrieve their scuba gear from the lighthouse. Then, in the *Sleuth,* they sped out to the marker buoy, where the salvage ship had already taken up its position.

Chet stood by, fascinated, while Frank and Joe donned rubber suits, flippers, masks, and breathing apparatus. Roland Perry was already encased in his diving dress on the stool, a red wool cap on his head.

"You're going in through the engine room?" Joe asked.

"I'll have to. The top hamper's all smashed and half buried in silt, the way she's lying. Remember now, you fellows take care."

"Aye, aye, sir." Frank grinned and saluted.

Perry's helmet was screwed on, the glass face-plate attached, and the air supply checked. Then he clumped onto the diving stage in his lead-weighted boots and was lowered into the water.

Meanwhile, Frank and Joe had pulled down their masks, inserted their mouthpieces, and tested their regulators. Both leaped over the side.

The Hardys cleaved their way steeply down-ward into the cold depths, trying to keep Perry in sight. The water darkened to a murky gray-green as they descended. At last the shattered hulk of the *Katawa* came in sight.

Both boys felt a chill of awe at their first view of the dead ship. Already coated with barnacles and scum, it lay upended on the ocean floor, stacks and superstructure rammed deeply into the mud. The high bow of the *Carona* had knifed clean through into the *Katawa*'s bridge and deckhousing, and the resultant wreckage had evidently crumpled fur-ther under the weight of the foundered vessel.

"No wonder Rollie has to go in through that hole in her side!" Joe thought.

The diver waved to them as he stepped off the platform, then plodded slowly toward the hulk, trailing his air hose and lifeline. The Hardys saw him close his outlet valve slightly to make his suit more buoyant so as to float himself upward toward the gaping hole. A startled school of fish came darting out as Perry made his way cautiously inside.

Frank and Joe swam closer. Dark swirls of oil were rising from the engine room, churned up by Perry's movements, and they could see little except the glow of his portable undersea lamp.

Meanwhile, the boys were flutter-kicking their way around the ship, peering at it from all sides. Somewhere in the sunken freighter was the strong room—did it still contain the gold Pharaoh's head?

The Hardys' air supply was getting low when Perry finally emerged. He made a thumbs-up gesture to return topside. Pausing at intervals to decompress, they made the ascent.

As soon as Frank and Joe were hauled aboard, they could see from the excited faces of the diving crew that Perry had telephoned important news from the wreck. The young sleuths waited impatiently until his helmet was removed.

"What's the dope, Rollie?" Joe asked eagerly.

"Whoever cut that hole in the *Katawa* stole her engine-room telegraph and tachometer—the only evidence that can prove who's responsible for the collision!"

CHAPTER XVI

Double Disappearance

"THE telegraph and tachometer—gone!"

Joe gave a startled whistle and glanced at Frank. The discovery of the missing instruments below boded ill for Transmarine Underwriters and could result in heavy claims!

Chet had already heard the diver's telephoned report from the bottom. "Say!" the stout lad spoke up. "Isn't there another telegraph and tachometer on the bridge?"

"Sure," said Perry, "but they wouldn't amount to much now, except scrap metal—even if I could pry them out. The bridge is nothing but a mass of junk, and the whole ship's perched right on top of it."

"How about the strong room?" Frank asked.

"That's probably pretty badly smashed, too," the diver said. "I couldn't get to it from the engine room—at least not yet. A lot of debris will have to be cleared away first."

The Hardy boys went below to change out of their scuba dress.

"What do you suppose Rollie will find when he gets to the strong room?" Joe mused aloud. "Think the gold Pharaoh's head is still there?"

"I don't know. Looks as if we'll have to wait a while to find out. The question is, Why were those indicators stolen?"

Joe shot his brother a surprised look. "That's obvious, isn't it? Whoever took them was trying to cover up responsibility for the collision."

"Maybe. It could also be a red herring—to cover up the theft of the head! Remember, the thief knew that hole in the *Katawa*'s side was bound to be seen by any salvage diver later on."

"Yes!" Joe said excitedly. "Then, if nothing was touched in the engine room, that would practically *prove* the thief had gone down for the head. Which, in turn, might touch off a big search by the police!"

"Right. So he may have figured that by misleading the insurance company, he'd have more time to dispose of the head safely."

"But all this is assuming the thief could get to the strong room," Joe pointed out.

"Rollie said the way to it is blocked."

"From the engine room it's blocked," Frank

corrected. "Maybe there's some other way to get at the room."

When the Hardys returned topside, they learned that Shane, Perry, and Captain Rankin were holding a meeting in the captain's cabin to map salvage plans. The three Bayporters were invited to attend.

Around the oval wooden table, Frank told his theory that the instrument thief's real objective might have been the Pharaoh's head.

"Is there any other way he could have reached the strong room?" the young sleuth asked.

Roland Perry hesitated. "He might have worked his way in through a deck hatch or companionway—I'd have to check. But offhand I doubt if that would have been any easier."

"Besides, lad," Captain Rankin put in, "would he have bothered to cut the hole in her side? The hole is the only tip-off that a thief was down there at all."

"That's true," Frank conceded.

"There could still be a reason," said Joe. "Maybe he figured the hole would throw us off the track for a while—at least long enough for him to sell the head."

Shane remarked wryly, "I'd say we're up against a pretty shrewd operator."

"Rollie," said Frank, "is there any chance the thief could have gotten the head—and *then* himself blocked access to the strong room?"

The three salvage men were startled by this idea.

"By George, I guess that's possible," Perry admitted. "With a small explosive blast, he might have shifted the debris inside the ship quite a bit. It'd be hard to tell now."

The Hardys and Chet exchanged quick glances. They had already found out—almost at the cost of their lives—that someone on Whalebone Island knew how to handle explosives!

"Well," Frank said, "to sum up, it looks as if there are four possible answers to the question of who cut that hole in the *Katawa*."

"Let's hear 'em," said Matt Shane.

"One: the thief may have been someone hired by the owners of the *Carona*, to help them duck responsibility for the collision. Two: he may have been a free-lance diver after the head—or maybe just after brass scrap. Three: he may have been hired by Mehmet Zufar, the owner of the head, to help him gyp the insurance company."

"You don't have to name the fourth," Perry broke in. "That I can already guess."

Joe nodded. "You mean Gus Bock?"

"I do. Bock's been my candidate for the thief ever since I first saw that hole."

"I realize Simon Salvage is not famous for square dealing," Captain Rankin said, frowning. "But do you believe even they'd risk such a maneuver?"

"Sure," Perry reasoned. "What else can they be doing around Whalebone Island? We know they wouldn't pass up any chance of big loot."

Before the discussion could continue, there was a knock on the door of the captain's cabin.

"Come in!" Rankin barked.

A deckhand stepped inside. "Sparks says there's a radiotelephone call from shore for the Hardy boys, Cap'n."

Frank and Joe excused themselves and hurried to the radio shack, Chet puffing along eagerly behind them. The call was from Sam Radley in Philadelphia.

"What's up, Sam?" Frank asked his father's operative.

"A couple of news items I thought I'd pass on to you fellows. For one thing, your dad has found out, through Interpol, who sent that warning cablegram from Egypt."

Frank's eyes lighted with interest. "Who?"

"The Egyptian police traced it to a Dutch gold-smith named Van Hoek who was living in Cairo."

"*Was* living?"

"That's right. He seems to have disappeared."

Frank glanced at Joe and Chet, who were listening in. Chet gulped.

"A goldsmith!" Joe exclaimed. "Sounds as if there might've been some funny business with the Pharaoh's head. Van Hoek may have made a duplicate!"

"And he may also be another victim of the Pharaoh's curse," Chet croaked gloomily.

"What's the rest of your news, Sam?" Frank asked, turning back to the telephone.

The detective hesitated before replying. "The truth is, your dad's missing, too. At least I haven't heard from him for over twenty-four hours."

"What! Haven't you any idea where he went?"

"None," Radley admitted worriedly, "except that he was following up on that lead from Zufar. Look, I'd rather not talk too much over the phone. Do you think you boys could break off what you're doing and fly here to Philadelphia?"

Alarmed for their father's safety, the Hardys readily agreed. Radley promised to arrange a special charter flight with the Ace Air Service, which would be standing by as soon as the youths could get back to Bayport.

Chet was sympathetic and immediately offered whatever assistance he could give his pals.

Frank gave him a grateful slap on the back. "Thanks, Chet. You've been a swell sport to help us this far. You deserve a break. We'll drop you off in Bayport, but stand by."

"You bet."

After a hasty farewell to their friends on the *Petrel*, the boys embarked in the *Sleuth*.

It was evening when they finally reached home. Here Frank and Joe ate a quick supper with Aunt Gertrude. Not wanting to worry her, they made no mention of Fenton Hardy's disappearance, saying only that they were needed urgently in Philadelphia to help on his current case.

"Any word from Mother?" Joe asked.

"Her friend is better, but Laura plans to stay on in Bartonsville a few days," Miss Hardy replied. "Don't eat so fast, boys! You're as bad as Tivoli."

Frank grinned. "How's Tivoli's appetite these days?"

"Humph! He does eat rather a lot, but he's proving to be a very well-behaved dog. I'm seeing to that!" Aunt Gertrude added with pride.

The two boys sped to the airport in their convertible and were soon taking off into the dusk aboard the charter plane.

Sam Radley met them at the Philadelphia air terminal, but waited until the Hardys were settled in a hotel room before telling them the whole story.

"When your dad and I opened that airport locker," he began, "we found a walkie-talkie inside."

"A walkie-talkie!" Frank exclaimed.

"Yes—with a note saying to keep listening in. But it wasn't till Saturday that anything came through."

"What did you hear?" Joe asked.

"Not much the first time. The voice that spoke sounded pretty suspicious—wanted to know why Zufar himself didn't answer. Your dad said he was acting as Zufar's agent or go-between for the pickup of the head."

"Then what?" Frank inquired.

"He was told to stand by for instructions—while the gang did some snooping around, I suppose, to make sure there was no trap."

"Then," Sam went on, "early yesterday morning another message came. Fenton was told this time to grab a taxi immediately, have the driver go down Market Street, and then turn north onto Johnson Avenue. The voice said he would receive further instructions en route."

The sandy-haired, muscular detective rose from his chair and paced anxiously about the room.

"I tried to follow him in another cab, but lost him in traffic. I haven't heard a word from him since."

Frank said, "Have you told the police?"

Radley nodded. "Yes, your father kept them informed all along, but there was no time to rig a trap. A police operator was tuned in on the same frequency, but he heard nothing."

"Some of the gang probably got close behind Dad's cab and broadcast at very low power, so the transmission wouldn't carry far," Joe declared.

Both boys felt sick with worry, but knew there was little they could do except await developments. Frank told Radley about Captain Early's cane and passed on the description of the "helpful" motorist and his car. Radley promised to have this circulated by the police.

"Better get some rest, fellows. We may need all our energy tomorrow," the operative advised after they had listened to the eleven-o'clock news report on TV.

Radley left to return to his own room. Frank and Joe undressed and went to bed. Exhausted by their strenuous day, they fell asleep quickly.

Joe awoke suddenly some time later. Was the floor creaking—or had he only imagined it? He raised his head from the pillow and peered around.

A shadowy figure was darting toward the window!

CHAPTER XVII

Secret of the Mummy Case

Joe was out of bed in a flash. He sprang clear across his brother's bed and leaped at the intruder in a flying tackle.

With a snarl, the man kicked backward. His heel connected full force with Joe's jaw and the boy crashed to the floor in a daze.

By this time Frank had awakened. He jumped out of bed just as the man was disappearing through the window. Frank ran over and stuck out his head. "Stop! Thief!" he yelled at the top of his lungs. The intruder was already darting down the fire escape into the pitch-dark alleyway below.

Frank raged in frustration. He had started to put on his bathrobe, in order to give chase. But he checked himself, not daring to leave Joe alone.

Dashing to the room telephone, he signaled the operator. "A man just broke into Room 321! He got away down the rear fire escape and went through the alley!"

Hurrying to his brother's assistance, Frank was relieved to find Joe groggily raising himself from the floor.

"Whoa! Easy, boy! Better stay put for a bit," Frank advised. He switched on the light, got Joe a glass of water, then helped him onto a bed.

"Feel okay?"

"Guess so. Slightly foggy, that's all." Joe waggled his jaw. "I guess it's not broken."

His eyes widened and he sat up again as Frank reached for a sheet of white paper propped on a table. "Our visitor left a message," said Frank.

"What's it say?"

Frank read aloud: " 'Leave town at once or there'll be trouble!' "

"More on the other side, isn't there?" Joe said.

When Frank turned the sheet over, his jaw tightened. Without a word, he handed the paper to Joe. The remainder of the message was:

AND DROP THE PHARAOH'S HEAD CASE IF YOU HOPE TO SEE YOUR FATHER AGAIN—ALIVE!

"If only I could've nailed that creep!" Joe complained bitterly.

"Did you get a look at him?"

"No, it all happened too fast." Joe scowled.

"But—there was something familiar about him, at that. Just his general shape, or the way he moved, I'm not sure what."

Frank went down the hall to rouse Sam Radley, whose room was several doors away. On the way back, they encountered the house detective.

"A couple of scout cars are cruising around, looking for likely suspects," the hotel security man reported. "Can you give us any description to go on?"

"Not a very good one, unfortunately," Frank said. "The man was tall and had on a dark suit, that's about all. He was pretty much in shadow going down the fire escape."

The house detective took down a complete account of the incident from both boys and offered the services of a doctor for Joe, who vigorously declined. "I'm fine, now."

Radley, meanwhile, had been prowling about the room, looking for clues. A moment after the hotel detective had left, Radley bent down and plucked something from behind the wastebasket near the window.

"Did either of you throw this away?"

The Hardys shook their heads. "What is it?" Frank asked.

"A notice of an art auction sale," Radley replied, holding out a small brochure, "from the Holt-Hornblow Galleries in New York."

"An art auction sale!" Joe exclaimed, looking at

his brother excitedly. "The fellow must have dropped it going out the window."

"That would figure, all right," Frank said. "If the men who kidnapped Dad really have the gold Pharaoh's head, they may be in the art business!"

They found no marks or jottings on the brochure which might provide a further clue.

"You know something?" Frank said suddenly. "There's an angle to this business we've been overlooking all along."

"What's that?" asked Radley.

"The gang behind all this must have had some real inside knowledge if they salvaged the head from the *Katawa*'s strong room. Remember, no story about the head being aboard was ever published in the newspapers."

Radley nodded. "True."

"One of the *Katawa*'s crew may have let the secret slip out," Frank went on. "Then word was passed along, either to a museum, or an art dealer —maybe someone who knows Zufar."

Joe suddenly leaped up off the bed as if he had been stung. "Sufferin' snakes!" he blurted. "Bogdan! Fritz Bogdan!"

"What?" Frank exclaimed.

"I mean, he was the man I saw—the guy who broke in tonight!"

Radley and Frank stared at Joe.

"How can you be sure," Radley asked, "if you didn't see his face?"

"I'm *not* sure," Joe admitted, "but at least I'm positive that's why the figure looked familiar. Tall, slightly stooped, right shoulder higher than the other—just like Bogdan!"

Frank was impressed by his brother's theory. "That definitely adds up," he said. "Bogdan could have learned from Zufar about the head going down on the *Katawa*—maybe heard about it the same day that it happened. So he decided to steal a march on the insurance company and hire somebody to grab it before they could send down a diver of their own."

"And remember, we suspected Bogdan was eavesdropping on us at Zufar's office," Joe said.

Sam Radley paced back and forth worriedly. "Boys, if you're right, we'd better move fast," he decided. "We might be able to nail Bogdan on his way back to New York from here."

"What's your plan, Sam?" Frank asked.

"We'll have police cover the airports, and the train and bus stations," the operative replied. "Meantime, we'll fly back to New York in our charter plane. If he's driving, we'll still get to New York before him."

The Ace Air Service pilot had planned to stay overnight at a motel near the Philadelphia airport. Sam telephoned him and arranged to have the plane readied for take-off immediately.

In less than an hour Radley and the boys were bound for La Guardia Airport.

As soon as they landed, they checked telephone directories to find Bogdan's home address, but could find no listing.

"Wait a second," Frank said. "Maybe Zufar can tell us."

He plucked out the art dealer's calling card. Zufar had jotted two telephone numbers on the back, along with the address of Bogdan's curio shop. One was the shop's number. The other proved to be that of Zufar's hotel.

A few moments after Frank had dialed it, Zufar's voice came hoarsely over the line, sounding as if he had just been awakened. "Yes? Who is calling?"

Frank explained the situation hastily. Zufar seemed to be flustered and incredulous at the idea that Bogdan might be involved in the Pharaoh's head plot. But he gave Frank the curio-shop proprietor's unlisted home number and address, which he said was an apartment not far from the shop.

"Let's try Bogdan by phone first," Joe suggested.

Frank called the number but got no response. Nor was there any answer from the shop number. The three sleuths hailed a taxi and sped into Manhattan.

Bogdan's apartment was on the first floor of an old converted brownstone. Its windows were dark, and the doorbell could be heard ringing hollowly inside.

"Maybe he hasn't come back from Philadelphia yet," Frank conjectured.

"We'd better keep a stakeout," said Radley. It was decided that he would remain on watch outside the brownstone while the Hardys covered the curio shop.

The boys taxied to the address and settled down to wait in an all-night drugstore across the street, which commanded a clear view of the shop entrance. The early morning passed slowly with no sign of Bogdan.

By ten o'clock neither the proprietor nor any of his employees had appeared to open the shop.

Finally Sam Radley arrived on the scene. Frank and Joe hurried across the street to meet him. The operative reported that he had called the Holt-Hornblow Galleries and confirmed the fact that a notice of the art auction sale had been sent to Fritz Bogdan. "I think we'd better call the police," Radley told the boys.

"Hold it!" Joe said. "Here's Zufar!"

The art dealer was just stepping out of a taxi. He looked upset at sight of the trio and twiddled his mustache nervously as they apprised him of the situation.

"Do you have a key to the shop?" Radley asked. When Zufar nodded, he went on, "Then suppose we go inside and search the premises."

"B-b-but we have no right to do that!" the dealer spluttered. "I merely occupy office space here as a favor from Bogdan."

"Look," Frank said angrily, "our dad was kidnapped carrying out a dangerous assignment for you. Your friend Bogdan may be behind the whole thing—including the theft of *your* golden Pharaoh's head."

Joe broke in. "We'll call the police and get a warrant."

Zufar fished out a silk handkerchief and daubed his perspiring face. "No, no—please! Let us do as you wish." He unlocked the front door of the shop and they went inside.

Radley made a hasty survey of the premises— showroom, offices, and storage space at the rear— to make sure that no one was about.

"What do you expect to find?" Zufar asked.

"Evidence," said Radley. "If Bogdan did mastermind this plot, the Pharaoh's head may be hidden here somewhere!"

The three sleuths began a thorough search. Would they find solid evidence linking Bogdan to the plot—and would it lead them to their missing father?

The boys and Sam probed into closets, crates, desks, rolled-up rugs—all in vain. Their hopes began to dwindle.

In the dusty showroom Frank paused and stared around despairingly. Once again, the faded, upright Egyptian mummy case caught his eye. On a sudden hunch, he strode toward it.

"Joe! Sam!"

His cry brought the others rushing over. Frank pointed to several tiny borings in the case. "These look like air holes!"

Together, the three pried at the mummy case, until Joe found a catch. When Frank and Sam wrenched off the lid, the trio gasped.

Wedged inside, with eyes closed, was the bound and gagged form of Fenton Hardy!

CHAPTER XVIII

Danger Below

THE boys were shocked at the sight of their father in the mummy case.

"Dad!" Joe cried in great alarm.

Frank felt Mr. Hardy's wrist and found a weak pulse. Carefully they eased the unconscious detective from the case.

"There's a sofa in Bogdan's office," said Sam. "Let's carry him in there."

They had taken only a few steps when Joe's eyes suddenly bulged. "That green Buddha!" he exclaimed.

"What's the matter?" Frank asked.

"Wait till we attend to Dad and I'll show you!"

The three laid Fenton Hardy on the sofa in Bogdan's office. Mehmet Zufar, visibly shaken, watched as Radley loosened the investigator's collar, then checked his respiration.

"I'd say he's been drugged," Sam declared. "We'd better get him to a hospital!"

While the operative telephoned for an ambulance and notified the police, Joe led Frank back to the Buddha figure.

"Take a look at that. Does anything about it strike you as odd?"

The large figure was coated with the pale-green patina of weathered bronze. It was seated in the "lotus" position, legs crossed, hands cupped in the lap.

Frank studied the Buddha intently for a moment. "Hmm. The head doesn't seem to match somehow—it's canted slightly to the left."

"Exactly. As if it was made separately from the body and then fitted on."

Frank's face suddenly lit up. "Jumpin' Jupiter! You think—?"

"I think this Buddha needs his skull X-rayed, that's what!"

As Joe seized the statue's head with both hands, Zufar came rushing up to the boys.

"*Ya khabar!*" he gasped. "What are you doing? You may damage the—"

"Relax, Mr. Zufar. If this is one-piece bronze, I can't damage it. If not—" As he spoke, Joe applied a slight twisting pressure to the statue's head.

Suddenly the neck seemed to move inside its tight-fitting necklace. An instant later the whole head came off in Joe's hands!

"You were right!" Frank shouted.

The lower portion of the neck, which had fitted

inside the necklace, showed none of the greenish bronze patina of the rest of the figure. Instead, it appeared to be hard-baked clay!

Frank lifted the head. "Wow! Heavy as lead!" he exclaimed. "The weight alone proves it was never part of the original hollow bronze casting." He turned it upside down to examine the base of the neck.

"Looks like solid clay," said Joe.

"It's clay, all right," Frank agreed. "The surface has been bronzed over and doctored with paint to give it the same weathered look as the body. But whether the clay's solid or not is another question."

"Let's find out!" Joe urged.

He lugged the head back to the storage room, followed by Frank and Zufar. Here Joe laid the head on a worktable, then picked up a hammer and chisel, evidently used for prying open crates.

"Wh-wh-what are you going to do?" Zufar stuttered, wringing his hands anxiously.

"See if this Buddha has a split personality." Joe poised the chisel on the head and gave it a sharp rap with the hammer. The face cracked and the clay fell away. They saw a yellow gleam of metal.

"The golden Pharaoh!" the boys cried out.

Zufar stared in stunned silence as the boys extricated the head from its broken clay shell. Frank and Joe were awed by the sheer beauty of the centuries-old statuette.

A tiny vulture and cobra protruded side by side from the Pharaoh's headdress. A long, slender goatee hung from the chin of the masklike golden face.

"Great Scott! What's going on!"

All three turned as Radley strode, wide-eyed, into the room. He told the boys that an ambulance was on the way, then they quickly related what had happened.

"The Pharaoh's head!" Sam exclaimed in astonishment. He turned to Zufar and asked, "Is it authentic?"

The perspiring art dealer lifted the object in trembling hands and examined it carefully.

"I should say it is unquestionably the same head that I was bringing to America—or, if not, the cleverest imitation I have ever seen. Of course, only a detailed examination by an expert Egyptologist—"

"Even that wouldn't prove it was the same one that went down on the *Katawa*, would it?" Joe broke in. "What if Rhamaton IV had two of these heads made—is that possible?"

Zufar shrugged. "Who can say?" Mopping his brow, the dealer added, "Anything is possible if my trusted friend and associate, Bogdan, could be party to such a villainous plot!"

The piercing wail of a siren came from the street outside. In a moment two ambulance at-

"The golden Pharaoh!" the Hardys cried out

tendants strode in, carrying a stretcher. Soon afterward, the police arrived.

Frank and Joe insisted on accompanying their father to the hospital. Radley elected to stay behind to acquaint the police with the situation.

"After we turn the Pharaoh's head over to the proper authorities, I'll meet you at the hospital," the operative promised.

It was past one o'clock in the afternoon and the Hardys had just finished eating a long-delayed breakfast in the hospital coffee shop when Radley finally rejoined them.

"How's your dad?" was his first question.

"Okay," Frank replied, "although he's still unconscious. The doctor says he was definitely drugged and he may not come out from the effects for hours."

Radley breathed a deep sigh of relief. The golden Pharaoh's head, he told the boys, had been entrusted to the Egyptology Department of the Metropolitan Museum for expert examination.

"Whew! This mystery is a real cliff-hanger!" Joe remarked. "I can hardly wait to find out what Perry will discover aboard the *Katawa*, too!"

The boys were torn between wanting to stay near their father and to keep an eye on the salvage operations as Mr. Hardy had wished.

Finally Radley convinced the two young sleuths to return to Whalebone Island.

"There's not much you fellows can do here except wait," he said. "So don't worry. I'll stick around till your dad revives."

Frank and Joe taxied to La Guardia where Sam's pilot was standing by. Soon they were winging their way to Bayport. Back home, Joe phoned Chet to bring him up to date and make plans for the island trip. Frank, meanwhile, told Aunt Gertrude of the recent events, then the brothers tumbled into bed.

The alarm clock awakened them at three o'clock the next morning. The boys showered, dressed, and hurried down to the kitchen to find a hearty breakfast of bacon and eggs awaiting them.

"You're a swell sport to get up just on our account, Aunt Gertrude," Frank said. "We sure appreciate it."

"Humph! Somebody has to see that you two get the proper nourishment," Miss Hardy said tartly, yet with a pleased look in her eyes.

The boys sped off in their convertible to the boathouse, where Chet soon joined them.

"I m-must be out of my mind to c-crawl out of the sack at this time of night!" he complained, shivering in the brisk, cool breeze of the bay.

"You wouldn't want to miss out on all the excitement, would you?" Joe said with a chuckle. "This may be the day we ferret out the final answer to the whole mystery—including the riddle of the Jolly Roger's ghost!"

Chet groaned loudly. "Now I *know* I should have stayed in bed!"

The *Sleuth* streaked out across Barmet Bay through the pre-dawn darkness. Late in the morning, they reached the *Petrel*, lying at the scene of the sinking, just north of Whalebone Island.

Roland Perry was resting on deck before going down for his second dive of the day.

"What's the picture, Rollie?" Joe asked.

"Better than we had any right to hope, fellows! I discovered the cargo had shifted enough so that I was able to cut a way through from the forward hold. Barring trouble, I should be able to get into the strong room itself on my next trip down!"

The Hardys and Chet were elated at the news.

"That'll be terrific!" Frank said enviously. "I wish we could be down there watching. Say, Rollie, did you do any salvage work for the Navy after the war?"

The diver nodded. "All along the coast here. A lot of ships are still resting on the bottom out in those waters. In fact, I remember seeing one enemy raider that your friend Captain Early accounted for."

"He must have been quite a skipper," Joe said admiringly.

"A real tiger, from the stories I've heard about him," Perry agreed. "Had four enemy ships to his credit—in the Atlantic. On that cane we gave him when he left the *Svenson*, the quartermaster carved the latitudes and longitudes of all four sinkings."

The Hardys stared at the diver.

"Latitudes and longitudes?" Frank echoed.

"Sure. You know—same as a fighter pilot painting his kills on the plane. We figured old Pearly Early had as much to boast about as any sky jockey."

The diver broke off as his tender and Matt Shane approached. "Looks as though it's time for my next dunk, fellows," Rollie said. "Stick around. I may have good news before the day's over."

The Bayporters walked off toward the rail while Sid Carter fitted the diving helmet over Perry's head.

Chet shot a quizzical glance at the Hardys. "What's up? I saw the way you both looked just now when Rollie mentioned the cane."

"Don't you get it?" said Joe.

"No," replied Chet. "Let me in on the secret."

"If Joe's thinking the same thing I am," said Frank, "the burglar who did those break-ins may have been after that information carved on the captain's cane—not his pearls at all."

"The location of those sinkings!"

"Right!" Joe turned to his brother. "You brought the cane along, didn't you, Frank?"

"Yes, it's in our boat. We'll take a look pronto!"

The three boys hurried across the deck and

climbed down into the *Sleuth,* which was moored alongside. Moments later, they were exclaiming in surprise as they studied the markings on the cane.

Joe reached into a locker and pulled out a map which he unfolded.

"Now we're getting somewhere," Frank remarked as he held the cane close and studied the latitude and longitude of Captain Early's first sinking. He read the numbers off carefully and Joe's finger swept across the map.

"Here it is! Off Newfoundland."

Frank read the next set of markings and Joe translated the position into a spot off North Carolina.

The next prey to the firepower of Captain Early's destroyer had been sunk ten miles off the New Jersey coast.

"Wow!" said Chet. "My history book says that was called the graveyard of the Atlantic!"

Frank had a little difficulty making out the latitude and longitude numbers representing the fourth sinking. Inscribed near the handle of the cane, they were dim from wear. Frank relayed the position, and as Joe pinpointed the location, he suddenly exclaimed, "Good night! That's right where we are!"

"Those lines nearly dissect Whalebone Island!" Chet said excitedly.

"I wonder what kind of craft the captain sent to Davy Jones's locker here," Joe remarked.

"Let's get hold of him on the radiotelephone," said Frank. "He can give us the answer."

At first there was no response. After several tries, however, Frank finally reached the officer.

"Captain Early!" he said excitedly. "That last bag made by your destroyer—was it off Whalebone Island?"

The boy heard the captain chuckle. "Yes, I guess it was. Our radar picked up that U-boat in the dead of night."

"A submarine?" Frank asked.

"Right! We dodged her torpedoes and sank her with ashcans—depth charges, that is. The enemy left an oil slick bigger than a circus tent. We found debris the next morning. A certain kill."

"Thanks a lot," said Frank. "That's great news, Captain. We'll tell you all about it later and return your cane, too."

Frank signed off and dashed out of the radio shack.

"You look as if you're about to jump out of your skin," said Joe.

"Boy, I am!" Frank exclaimed, and told about the German sub.

"Then you mean—?" Joe's question was broken off by the high-pitched voices of excited crewmen running toward them.

"What's wrong, Sid?" Joe asked Perry's tender.

"An explosion down below!"

"Good night! Was Rollie hurt?"

"Doesn't seem to be from what he said on the phone," Carter replied. "We're not sure just what happened. He's on his way up now."

Tension ran high on the *Petrel* as the crew waited out Perry's gradual ascent. Finally he was hauled out of the water.

"Sure you're okay, Rollie?" Matt asked as the diver's helmet was removed.

Perry's face was flushed with rage. "Not a scratch—but it was sheer luck!" The diver related that as he was about to enter the *Katawa*'s hold, he had sighted a huge squid which had apparently come prowling into the hulk. Perry had backed off to give it a wide berth. As he waited outside the sunken freighter for the squid to swim away, a sudden small explosion blew the creature to fragments!

Perry went on, tight-lipped, "Must have been a booby trap planted near the edge of the hold —gelignite, probably—and the squid brushed against it. Could've been me—which was probably the idea of whoever set the trap. Or, if I hadn't touched it off myself, my air line would have, while I was moving around inside. You know what that would have done!"

The boys grimaced. With a sudden loss of compression from a ruptured air hose, the diver would have been crushed to a jelly inside his helmet by the ocean pressure!

"Get this suit off me fast, Sid!" Perry directed, grim-faced.

Matt Shane looked apprehensive. "What are you going to do, Rollie?"

"I've got a score to settle with someone, Matt, and I aim to do it right now!"

"Hold on!" Captain Rankin stepped forward and gripped the diver's shoulder. "If you're implying Gus Bock's responsible for the explosive, you have no proof!"

"I don't need proof!" Perry growled. "You heard him threaten me the other night. Who else could've set that booby trap—the squid?"

Both Shane and Rankin pleaded in protest, but Perry refused outright to continue diving until he had dealt with Bock.

Finally the two older men agreed to accompany him to the *Simon Salvor* for a showdown. The Hardys volunteered to take them to the other salvage ship in the *Sleuth*. Chet, too, went along.

Moments later, they drew up alongside the *Salvor*. There was no attempt to block the party from the *Petrel* as they climbed aboard.

But the boys noticed a strange air of tension and anxiety among the *Salvor* crewmen who faced them.

"We weren't expecting visitors, Mr. Rankin," said the *Salvor*'s skipper coldly. "What's on your mind?"

"An explosive was planted on the *Katawa* by someone who wanted to kill our master diver," Rankin replied. "Perry here thinks Gus Bock had something to do with it."

"Where is he?" Perry spoke up harshly. "I'll tell him what I've come to say—face to face!"

"Not on this deck you won't," the skipper said. "Gus is not here."

"Then where is he?"

The eyes of the *Salvor* captain focused on the water. "Trapped on the bottom. He'll be lucky to see daylight again!"

CHAPTER XIX

Strong-Room Surprise

Gus Bock trapped! The Hardys and Chet were startled. Roland Perry stared in disbelief.

"Don't give us that," the diver snarled. "Bock may be on the bottom, but he'll come up again. We'll wait till he does."

"You'll have a long wait, then," the *Salvor's* captain retorted.

"We'll wait," Perry maintained.

"Anyhow, you're barking up the wrong tree. The only way one of our hands could have gotten to the *Katawa* is with scuba gear. And neither Bock nor anyone else has been off this ship except in a hardhat at the end of an air hose—not since the night he went ashore on Whalebone with Kraus."

As he spoke, the captain jerked his thumb toward the baldheaded man with sandy eyebrows whom the Hardys had seen outside the cave with

Bock. "Go ahead and talk to Gus on the phone if you don't believe me."

"Might as well, Rollie," Frank advised.

Perry scowled uncertainly for a moment; then, accompanied by the others, strode around the afterdeck to the opposite side of the ship where the diving crew was stationed.

He took a headset from one of the tenders and spoke into the microphone.

"This is Perry, Bock. You in trouble down there?"

Bock's voice came back weakly over the speaker, "What do *you* care?"

"Answer me!"

"All right, I'm pinned, if you want to know. Come on down and help me feed the fishes."

"I'll be down, don't worry—just so I can settle a score with you, once we get topside again!"

Perry turned to the Simon company's salvage master. "What happened?"

"Like Gus told you—he's pinned. Our apprentice diver Ryan is trying to help him, but it looks hopeless."

"Got another diving suit aboard?" Perry asked.

The *Salvor*'s captain said brusquely, "Forget it, Perry. You're not going down there."

"There is nothing you can do," Kraus added in his guttural accent.

Frank sensed another reason for the men's strange attitude. "If you aim to keep us from finding out what you've been working on," he spoke up, "you're out of luck. We've already learned there's a German sub down there."

Frank's words seemed to fall like a bombshell. Kraus and the *Salvor*'s skipper gaped at him in dismay.

"Now how in thunder do you figure that, son?" asked Matt Shane.

"From the American captain who sank her," Frank said. "I guess you never knew it happened so close to Whalebone, Rollie," he added. "That was before you joined the *Svenson*."

Perry turned to the Simon salvage master, Fosburg. "Okay, you heard him. What's the picture?"

Fosburg explained that the shattered U-boat had been lying on its side. Its stern was sunk deep in the muck and its bow was tilted upward, resting on the ledge of an undersea reef. But an explosive charge which Bock had set off inside the sub earlier that morning had partially dislodged it.

On his next dive, the wreck had suddenly slipped off the ledge completely. Bock had been pinned under a flap of hull metal.

"It's gradually squashing him downward as the ship settles into the silt," Fosburg ended grimly. "Ryan says it's only a question of time till he's crushed or his suit punctures."

"Can't you take a purchase on the bow and hoist it enough to free him?" Perry asked.

The salvage master shook his head. "Bock's lying under the after edge of the flap. Raising the bow would just push him down worse. The only way would be to parbuckle the whole U-boat so's to raise the keel—but there's not a chance of getting wires under her. Not in time, anyhow."

"Then what about cutting away the flap with a torch?"

"Too dangerous. Bock was carrying another charge of explosive and dropped it when the hulk fell on him. Dynamite and primacord, all set to blow if the flame comes anywhere near it!"

"Then what're you going to do—let him die?" Perry flared angrily.

The salvage master shrugged. "Ryan's afraid to risk it. Personally, I don't blame him."

"Then break out a cutting torch and another diving rig—I'll do it myself!" Perry snapped.

Fosburg called down to Bock to ask if he would agree.

"You kidding?" the trapped diver called back. "What have *I* got to lose!"

Perry dropped the phone and instantly suited up.

The Hardys and Chet waited, tense and silent, as Perry made his descent. For a time there was no word from him after he reached the bottom.

Then his voice came over the deck speaker!

"There may be another way to do this, Fosburg. Ask Frank and Joe Hardy if they're willing to come down with face masks and air lines."

Both boys quickly volunteered to do so, and were informed the air lines also contained a phone connection.

Perry went on, "Have each of them bring down an iron needle with a hoisting wire attached to it."

Removing their clothes, Frank and Joe donned skin-diving suits from the *Sleuth* and special face masks from the *Salvor*'s diving locker. Meanwhile, the needles had been laid out on deck—each a huge iron rod with a wire rope shackled to an eye at one end. The rods were lowered over the side, with Frank and Joe clinging to them. Then the wires were payed out slowly.

The green ocean water grew darker and dimmer as they descended. At last, like a still, ghostly monster, the long, slim hulk of the dead U-boat could be made out on the bottom.

Perry and Ryan—the *Salvor*'s apprentice diver —stood waiting for them.

The Hardys felt an ominous chill of fear as they saw Bock's helmet and shoulders extending out from under the jagged flap of metal below the keel.

Fosburg transmitted Perry's orders over the boys' phone lines. "He wants those needles jammed way under the flap. Frank, you help Ryan with one rod—and, Joe, help Perry."

With grunting effort, the four divers at last got the needles wedged into position. Then Perry's voice reached the crew on deck:

"Okay, put a strain on those wires!"

As winches heaved the wires taut, the rods slowly came upright, levering the metal flap upward. In moments the rescuers had pulled Bock free!

Then came the long, slow ascent back to the *Simon Salvor*. Safe on deck with his helmet off, Bock gasped out his thanks.

"Still want to break my neck, Rollie?"

Perry, somber-faced, shook his head. "Not yet, anyhow. Too much trouble saving it. Just tell me one thing—did you have anything to do with a gelignite booby trap on the *Katawa?*

The rescued diver swore fervently that he knew nothing about it. "Haven't been near her. I'll admit I was the frogman who slipped the *Petrel*'s anchor—but that's all. And listen, Perry. About that old score you've been wanting to settle—believe me, I didn't try to cut your air line."

"Okay, Gus. I'll take your word."

Bock stuck out his huge paw. "I'm willing to call it quits."

"Guess I go along with that," said Perry, shaking hands.

"Now," Frank said to Bock, "how about telling us what you fellows are after aboard the U-boat?"

The diver opened his mouth to reply, but Kraus cut him off sharply. "Tell them nothing, Bock! *Nothing*—do you hear?"

"Shut up, Kraus!" Bock retorted. "These guys

saved my life. I'm not only gonna tell 'em—we're gonna cut 'em in, see?''

Ignoring Kraus's protests, he turned back to the boys and Perry. "You know what's down in that sub? Five hundred grand in American currency—that's what—a cool half million!"

Chet's eyes grew big as saucers, and the Hardys were just as startled as their chum.

"A half million—how do you know?" Perry asked Bock.

"Kraus here was a torpedoman on it!"

Bock went on to explain that in the closing months of World War II a group of top Nazis had fled Germany aboard the U-511 with a fortune in American currency.

"Heading where—to South America?" Frank broke in.

"Right—until steering trouble and dogged pursuit by Allied sub-killers took them far off course."

The U-boat had then hove to off Whalebone Island for repairs one night and sent a reconnaissance party ashore.

"Kraus got separated from the party and was stranded when his mates were suddenly called back to the ship."

"Because of the *Svenson!*" Chet spoke up.

Bock nodded. "The Germans sighted Captain Early's destroyer. Then the *Svenson* engaged the U-511 and sank her, but Kraus thought it got away."

"So *Kraus* was the red-bearded apparition who scared the wits out of Tang, the lighthouse keeper!" put in Joe.

Bock chuckled. "You guessed it, kid. He hid in a cave and finally got to the mainland in a boat swiped from a fisherman."

Kraus, the boys learned, had met Bock by chance years later. An exchange of information between the two had led to the present salvage effort.

"I remembered the sinking," Bock went on, "and knew that Captain Early's cane gave the exact location."

In response to further questioning by the Hardys, Bock admitted his group was responsible for the various break-ins and the highway incident involving Captain Early's car. But their search for the sunken submarine had been fruitless until their prowler came upon Early's carved cane at the Hardy house.

"That's the guy right over there," Bock said, pointing to a muscular member of the salvage crew. "You won't hold it against him, will you?"

Frank and Joe shook their heads. "No hard feelings as long as you're giving us the whole story," said Frank. "But Kraus will have to square himself with immigration authorities."

Bock, however, denied any knowledge of the "ghost" at the Hardys' house or the island explosion trap.

"Then why did you threaten Dad?" Joe asked.

"I was plenty sore that he kept us from getting the salvage contract for the *Katawa*," Bock admitted. "It would've given us swell cover for this job and kept you guys out of our hair. Right now, I'm sure glad you were around!"

The *Petrel* party, eager to resume their own diving operation, soon headed back in the *Sleuth* to their ship.

It was nightfall when Perry telephoned electrifying news from the bottom: He had succeeded in forcing an entry to the *Katawa's* strong room!

"What about the head?" Frank called down tensely.

"It's here, all right. At least there's a case that looks like the one the insurance company described—and there's something heavy inside!"

Some time later, a breathless group gathered in Captain Rankin's cabin. On the desk lay a metal carrying case. Frank, acting for his father as the representative of Transmarine, was allowed to open it. Inside was an object wrapped in green velvet cloth.

"J-j-jeepers! Unwrap it quick!" Chet urged.

Frank stripped away the velvet cloth, revealing a gleaming gold head.

"Is it the real McCoy?" Perry asked.

"Sure looks like it," Frank murmured. He hesitated, then took out his jackknife and made a tiny scratch in the base of the statuette.

Grayish metal could be seen beneath the gold!

"It's gilded lead!" Joe cried out. "A fake!" He stopped short as sudden confused noises and shouts were heard on deck.

"What's going on out there?" Captain Rankin exclaimed. He and the others sped from the cabin. As they reached the deck, the five shielded their eyes and staggered. Dense clouds of fuming vapor were billowing over the deck!

"Tear gas!" Frank gasped. "Look—those men!"

Near the glowing deckhouse, ghostly figures with gas masks could be seen darting about, swinging clubs and blackjacks! *Petrel* crewmen rushing topside were promptly clubbed as they came on deck.

"We've—got—to stop them!" Joe yelled, his eyes stinging with pain. He groped forward past a fallen sailor, then felt himself roughly thrown to the deck.

Frank and Chet battled valiantly. But an instant later they were seized from behind in a grip of iron. Half-blinded and choking, the boys were helpless!

Soon the entire *Petrel* crew was subdued. Many, including Roland Perry, were unconscious. Frank, Joe, Chet, Captain Rankin, and one other man stood on deck with their hands tied.

"But who—?" Frank murmured to himself.

Dazed, the captive group squinted through the

darkness as two of the mystery raiders approached them.

When they removed their masks, the Hardys gasped.

"Mehmet Zufar!" Joe cried out. "And Fritz Bogdan!"

The fat, mustached art dealer rubbed his hands and sneered triumphantly. Then he commanded, "Captain, you will now hand over the head which your diver brought up from the sunken *Katawa* before—"

"Before what?" Captain Rankin snapped back.

Zufar chuckled and glanced over the rail at the dark water.

"Before," he whispered, "we—as you say—scuttle this ship and send you all to the bottom!"

CHAPTER XX

Rhamaton's Curse

"THIS is piracy!" Captain Rankin exploded. "Piracy and murder! You'll all pay for it with your lives!"

Zufar twirled his mustache smugly. "Ah, but no, my dear captain—not with all the evidence lying on the bottom of the ocean. Your ship will disappear without a trace."

"Don't count on that!" Rankin stormed. "Chances are my radioman got off a call for help before you thugs took over."

"I hate to disillusion you." Zufar smiled. "But your radioman has been in my pay all along. He has been most useful to us."

"Harry Egner? I don't believe it!"

"It is true, nevertheless. He, of course, will die with you, now that his usefulness is at an end."

The Hardys clenched their fists, forgetting fear in their anger at being trapped. Chet Morton threw them a despairing glance.

Frank's jaw tightened. He thought, "We'll have to play for time." In a loud voice he asked Zufar, "How did you and your gang get here?"

"From a coastal hideout," Zufar replied with a gloating smirk. "As soon as Egner radioed us that the Rhamaton head was on the way up from the *Katawa*, we lost no time."

Bogdan put in boastfully, "Thanks to my idea of using tear gas, our task was made easier."

Frank ignored the curio dealer and kept his eyes fixed on Zufar. "You had to keep the fake head from coming into the hands of the insurance company, is that it?"

"Exactly. Even though you and your brother detected the authentic head in New York, I still look forward to collecting one million dollars insurance from Transmarine Underwriters, you see."

"But why were you shipping the fake in the first place?" Chet asked. "You couldn't have known beforehand the *Katawa* would sink in a collision."

"To palm it off on somebody!" Joe put in.

"Quite so. I intended to sell the—er—reproduction to a wealthy South American collector—whose agent had examined the original in Beirut." Zufar laughed. "Clever? At any rate, I felt the chance of doubling my profits was worth the risk."

Meanwhile, Zufar explained, the real head had been sent on to Bogdan to sell secretly elsewhere.

"Then came the sinking." The art dealer shook

his head sadly. "But it enabled me, of course, to claim a million dollars in insurance—if the fake head were never salvaged."

"So you sent down your own diver?" Frank interjected.

"Exactly. But unfortunately our man was unable to get through to the strong room before the *Petrel* arrived."

Captain Rankin, who had been standing grim-faced, now broke out in an angry voice, "Then Frank and Joe were right! You took out the telegraph and tachometer instead—as a cover-up for the hole in the *Katawa* hull!"

At this, Bogdan stuck his face close to the Hardys. "Smart kids! We'll see how smart you are when we sink you forty fathoms under!"

Chills crawled up the boys' spines, but Frank, undaunted, pressed further. "Who was your diver?"

Zufar pointed to a swarthy, thickset man. One of Bogdan's employees! He chuckled. "And also the 'ghost' who gave you such a hard time on Whalebone Island."

Joe glared at the diver. "So you blinked the signals, conked our Dad, and set off the explosion."

It was further learned that he also had stolen Lawson's rental boat, left the warning note, ransacked Mr. Hardy's camp, and stove the hole in his boat.

Zufar went on, "Our diver's 'ghost' camouflage was quite useful, since he had to stay on the island while working on the *Katawa*. He returned, you see, after you left the island the first time."

"What about the ghost we saw at home?" Joe put in.

"That was me," Bogdan spoke up.

"So there were two of you playing the ghost game," said Frank.

"Yes," Bogdan replied. "It was another of my brilliant ideas. I had heard the legend of Whalebone Island, and thus thought of reviving Red Rogers' spirit."

"No wonder you looked familiar the first time we saw you at your shop!" Frank muttered.

Joe glared at the grinning art dealer and his cohorts. "You're a slick actor, Zufar! I suppose the broken-cat business with Mr. Scath was just an act to set the stage for my father's kidnapping."

"Mostly that—but also, partly, to make myself appear innocent of any hint of fraud."

Frank spoke up, "That gelignite booby trap on the *Katawa* this morning—did your man plant it?"

Zufar nodded. "Thanks to Egner's timely warning by radio that your diver was close to the strong room. A pity it failed."

"How about the warning cablegram from Cairo?" Joe said. "Was Van Hoek in your pay too?"

"Not only that—he made our counterfeit Pharaoh's head. We hoped the cablegram might serve as a false lead, perhaps even frighten your father off the case." Zufar sneered. "Unfortunately, Van Hoek himself is a superstitious fool! The thought of the Pharaoh's curse began to prey on his mind and he finally fled from Cairo. We have lost track of him."

"We're wasting time, gabbing with these brats, Zufar!" Bogdan snarled. "Let's open the seacocks and sink this tub!"

"Quite right, quite right, my friend. But first we must have these five drag their shipmates below. It will be much better, I think, if no bodies float to the surface."

"Oh yeah?" a harsh voice broke in. "Maybe that's what you bilge rats will be doin' when *we* get through with you!"

Men were suddenly swarming over the rail!

Joe let out a yelp of joy. "It's Gus Bock and his buddies!"

The burly diver leaped aboard, with fists swinging. Kraus, Fosburg, Ryan, and the *Salvor's* captain joined the fray. Bock paused long enough to free the Hardys and the others.

Zufar's henchmen, stunned by the swift turn of events, fought back, wildly brandishing their weapons.

"Stop them! Stop them!" the fat ringleader

shrilled, his voice rising hysterically. The next instant Bock seized him and drew back a mighty fist. Zufar begged for mercy. "D-don't hit me! I give up."

Frank spotted Bogdan about to swing himself over the rail. The young sleuth leaped toward him and pinioned the curio dealer's arms. Kraus, nearby, sent a rocketing uppercut to the jaw of the "ghost" diver, who crumpled to the deck.

Joe and Chet had succeeded in disarming and capturing two more of the enemy.

Finally Zufar's gang were completely subdued. By this time most of the *Petrel*'s unconscious crewmen had revived. Roland Perry also had come to.

With Zufar, Bogdan, and the other prisoners tied and locked in a cabin, warm handshakes were exchanged between the *Petrel*'s men and their rescuers.

"Looks as though we're all square now—eh, Gus?" Perry said with a grin.

"Who says, bubblehead?" Bock retorted. "I told you we were gonna cut you guys in on the U-boat dough and we are! In fact, we were just bringin' it over to you when we got wind of what was goin' on aboard."

He emptied a canvas bag onto the captain's desk. The Hardys and Chet gasped as bundles of water-soaked green currency came tumbling out!

"There you are, pals! Your share—a hundred

grand. Divvy it up any way you like. The stuff got a bit water-logged in the chest, but you can still spend it."

Perry and his mates stared in astonishment, unable to find words. Then Frank peeled off a soggy bill and held it up.

"Careful," Bock advised. "That dough's been down in Davy Jones's locker so long it almost comes apart in your fingers."

Frank nodded, kneading the fibers of the bill. "I know—that's what I want it to do. Gus, unless I'm off-base, this money's counterfeit, probably manufactured by the Nazis themselves."

"What!" Bock seemed on the verge of apoplexy.

Joe inspected the bill. "I think Frank's right," he said. "We once helped our dad in a case involving counterfeit money and learned a few pointers about detecting phony currency. One way is from the paper itself. I'll bet anything this isn't the same composition as paper used for American money."

Bock stared glassy-eyed at his companions. At first the Hardys thought he might put his fist through the bulkhead in sheer rage. But suddenly the big diver tossed his head back and burst into bellows of laughter.

"What a bunch of saps we are! All that trouble we went to, and the dough turns out to be fake!"

Kraus could only shake his head and mutter, *"Ach du lieber Himmel!"*

"We could be wrong," Frank said.

"Somehow I got a feeling you ain't." Bock slapped him on the back. "But never mind, we'll all hang onto this funny money till we find out for sure."

A little later the Hardys contacted Sam Radley. They were overjoyed to learn their father had fully recuperated and would be out of the hospital the next day. Sam assured the boys he would give Mr. Hardy full details of their sleuthing success.

"Splendid work, fellows," the operative added.

Two days later Fenton Hardy confirmed his sons' verdict about the money when he and Sam Radley boarded the *Petrel* at its pier in New York.

"Bock and Kraus aren't the only ones who were misled," Mr. Hardy added. "That goldsmith Van Hoek is now under arrest."

"No kidding!" Joe exclaimed. "Where'd they nail him, Dad?"

"In Amsterdam, on several counts of art forgery. He stepped off the plane from Cairo and walked straight into the arms of the Dutch police."

Chet flashed a wise look at his two chums. "When you received the secret warning I had a hunch the Pharaoh's curse was no laughing matter. It sure caught up with Zufar and his gang." He hooked his thumbs into his belt. "Now that this case is closed," he said with an air of satisfaction, "we can relax a little. Hey! How about going to Captain Early's place and—"

"Eating more juicy lamb chops, I suppose," Joe put in with a quick smile.

"Aw! Quit reading my mind!"

"Wait! Chet has a point," Frank concluded. "I think Captain Early should get a firsthand report of the final salvo."

"And I'll present the cane," Chet said.

With a victory whoop, the boys set off, unaware at the moment that *The Twisted Claw*, their next mystery, soon would plunge them into another harrowing adventure.

ORDER FORM

HARDY BOYS MYSTERY SERIES

Now that you've seen Frank and Joe Hardy in action, we're sure you'll want to read more thrilling Hardy Boys adventures. To make it easy for you to purchase other books in this exciting series, we've enclosed this handy order form.

55 TITLES AT YOUR BOOKSELLER
OR COMPLETE AND MAIL THIS
HANDY COUPON TO:

GROSSET & DUNLAP, INC.
P.O. Box 941, Madison Square Post Office, New York, N.Y. 10010

Please send me the Hardy Boys Mystery and Adventure Book(s) checked below @ $1.95 each, plus 25¢ per book postage and handling. My check or money order for $_____ is enclosed.

#	Title	Code		#	Title	Code
1.	Tower Treasure	8901-7		28.	The Sign of the Crooked Arrow	8928-9
2.	House on the Cliff	8902-5		29.	The Secret of the Lost Tunnel	8929-7
3.	Secret of the Old Mill	8903-3		30.	Wailing Siren Mystery	8930-0
4.	Missing Chums	8904-1		31.	Secret of Wildcat Swamp	8931-9
5.	Hunting for Hidden Gold	8905-X		32.	Crisscross Shadow	8932-7
6.	Shore Road Mystery	8906-8		33.	The Yellow Feather Mystery	8933-5
7.	Secret of the Caves	8907-8		34.	The Hooded Hawk Mystery	8934-3
8.	Mystery of Cabin Island	8908-4		35.	The Clue in the Embers	8935-1
9.	Great Airport Mystery	8909-2		36.	The Secrets of Pirates Hill	8936-X
10.	What Happened At Midnight	8910-6		37.	Ghost at Skeleton Rock	8937-8
11.	While the Clock Ticked	8911-4		38.	Mystery at Devil's Paw	8938-6
12.	Footprints Under the Window	8912-2		39.	Mystery of the Chinese Junk	8939-4
13.	Mark on the Door	8913-0		40.	Mystery of the Desert Giant	8940-8
14.	Hidden Harbor Mystery	8914-9		41.	Clue of the Screeching Owl	8941-6
15.	Sinister Sign Post	8915-7		42.	Viking Symbol Mystery	8942-4
16.	A Figure in Hiding	8916-5		43.	Mystery of the Aztec Warrior	8943-2
17.	Secret Warning	8917-3		44.	Haunted Fort	8944-0
18.	Twisted Claw	8918-1		45.	Mystery of the Spiral Bridge	8945-9
19.	Disappearing Floor	8919-X		46.	Secret Agent on Flight 101	8946-7
20.	Mystery of the Flying Express	8920-3		47.	Mystery of the Whale Tattoo	8947-5
21.	The Clue of the Broken Blade	8921-1		48.	The Arctic Patrol Mystery	8948-3
22.	The Flickering Torch Mystery	8922-X		49.	The Bombay Boomerang	8949-1
23.	Melted Coins	8923-8		50.	Danger on Vampire Trail	8950-5
24.	Short-Wave Mystery	8924-6		51.	The Masked Monkey	8951-3
25.	Secret Panel	8925-4		52.	The Shattered Helmet	8952-3
26.	The Phantom Freighter	8926-2		53.	The Clue of the Hissing Serpent	8953-X
27.	Secret of Skull Mountain	8927-0		54.	The Mysterious Caravan	8954-8
				55.	The Witchmaster's Key	8955-6

SHIP TO:

NAME _____
(please print)

ADDRESS _____

CITY _____ STATE _____ ZIP _____